"With *Win Me Something*, Kyle Lucia Wu tenderly and masterfully reveals the fury, hope, and longing that come with trying to be seen in a world that never looks for you."

—MIRA JACOB,
author of *Good Talk*

"In *Win Me Something*, Kyle Lucia Wu examines the biracial experience with razor-sharp precision, nuance, and profound feeling. Her prose radiates off the page, with every color, character, and scrap of food animating the world of this story, all of it asking who, and what, is of value in America? I love the gentle candor of Wu's prose, the sneaky devastation. Her debut is a resonant knockout."

—T KIRA MADDEN,
author of *Long Live the Tribe of Fatherless Girls*

"Kyle Lucia Wu's *Win Me Something* is groundbreaking in its exploration of blended families and a biracial Asian American consciousness. In subtle but strikingly observed scenes that depict race, class, and lives of having and not having, she explores the secret want that we all have: to belong to something, somewhere. Here we find Willa, a biracial Chinese American narrator seeking to understand where she belongs in the family of things. Here is a prose writer who relishes in the poetry of language. Under Wu's deft hand, each sentence unfolds like a miracle."

—CATHY LINH CHE,
author of *Split*

"Taut, engrossing, and masterfully observed, *Win Me Something* announces a powerful and luminescent new literary voice in Kyle Lucia Wu."

—ALEXANDRA KLEEMAN,
author of *Something New Under the Sun*

"Like a latter-day Willa Cather, after whom her protagonist is named, Kyle Lucia Wu has written a beautiful novel about a fiercely American young woman whose Americanness is constantly questioned by those around her. This is a sad, funny, and tender coming-of-age story about what family and belonging means for someone who is realizing that she is constantly watched but not truly seen."

—DAVID BURR GERRARD,
author of *The Epiphany Machine*

"*Win Me Something* is an observant, contemplative story about the complex reality of growing up with a mixed identity in two starkly different mixed families. Kyle Lucia Wu deftly weaves back and forth between Willa's teenaged years and her adult life to explore loneliness, uncertainty, and a singular, persistent question—where do I truly belong?"

—CRYSTAL HANA KIM,
author of *If You Leave Me*

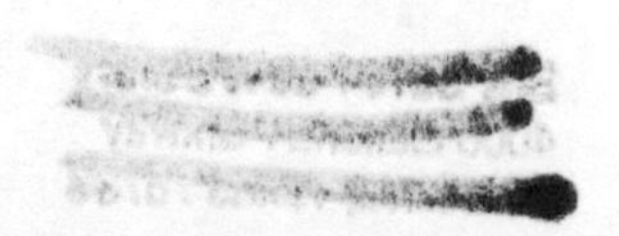

Win Me Something

KYLE LUCIA WU

TIN HOUSE / Portland, Oregon

Published by Tin House, Portland, Oregon

Distributed by W. W. Norton & Company

Library of Congress Cataloging-in-Publication Data

Names: Wu, Kyle Lucia, 1989- author.
Title: Win me something / Kyle Lucia Wu.
Description: Portland, Oregon : Tin House, [2021]
Identifiers: LCCN 2021019392 | ISBN 9781951142735 (paperback) |
ISBN 9781951142810 (ebook)
Subjects: LCSH: Chinese Americans—Fiction. | Families—Fiction. |
GSAFD: Bildungsromans.
Classification: LCC PS3623.U285 W56 2021 | DDC 813/.6—dc23
LC record available at https://lccn.loc.gov/2021019392

First US Edition 2021
Printed in the USA
Interior design by Jakob Vala

www.tinhouse.com

For my dad, and his love of books
For my mom, and her love of flowers

It seems so selfish, to want to be known!

—Yanyi, *The Year of Blue Water*

1

New York City, 2013

I didn't know what it looked like to take care of someone. I imagined that being a nanny meant watching a small person bounce her backpack home from school, microwaving chicken nuggets on a paper-toweled plate, and lying with an arm folded behind my head while the bright colors of a cartoon flashed. The intricacies of it hadn't occurred to me—that I'd have to sniff her palms to discern the citrus scent of soap and scrape dirt from underneath her fingernails. How I'd end up eating a room-temperature scoop of macaroni and cheese off her plate and raking lice shampoo through her soapy scalp. Maybe I couldn't imagine these moments because when someone asked about my childhood, my mind clenched and closed like two fists in a pool—fingers squeezing for something to come up with when everything around them was a different kind of matter.

I had parents. I had siblings. I had homes, multiple or zero, depending on how you looked at it. I wasn't unloved, not uncared for, exactly. It was cloudier than that, ink spreading in water as I tried to claim the words. If you're undercared for, but essentially fine, what do you do with all that hurt, the kind that runs through your tendons and tugs on your muscles, but doesn't show up on your skin? There were harder things in the world, hundreds of them. I floated silently through.

*

It was a swampy day in early August when I interviewed with the Adriens. I stood in front of my window unit damply, asking the cool air to soak me up. I picked out my most conservative dress, navy-blue cotton that reached just above my knees. It had straps that I thought too flimsy for the occasion, so I dug out a whispery, pale yellow cardigan from the back of my dresser drawer—something I'd bought on sale, thinking I might have a professional opportunity to wear it to. And now I did, in Tribeca at two o'clock.

I had only a muddy sense of why I was going. I sank into an orange seat and felt the train lurch forward, at home in my unease. It seemed like I often sat still while the pieces of my life rearranged around me, my only job to be stoic and unmoved, to come up for air and readjust once they stopped shifting. But there was a reason for this interview, I reminded myself: a move out of one service industry into another, a change of hours from late nights working the bar or early mornings at the coffee shop, to afternoons and early evenings—hours to make a life around. That appealed to me. The idea of opening my day up to something more—to echo the sleeping patterns of the rest of the city, to chisel out some vision for my future self—the hope that it might find me.

*

The lobby held no trace of the heat wave. A uniformed doorman held open one of the wide glass doors and the glacial air urged me in. I told him I was here to see the Adriens.

"Willa, right?" he said, kindly. "They're expecting you." He walked me to the elevator, and I stepped inside, wanting to stay for a moment before pressing the button, but then I saw him turn a key and press the number 5 before moving back into the lobby. After one short whoosh, the doors opened again, and Nathalie was standing in her entryway. Even though I knew they had the whole floor, I wasn't expecting to be inside their home so quickly. I stepped off the elevator, the sun in my eyes, and held my hand up like a visor. I felt the slipperiness of my underarms and elbows and backs of my knees, prickled by the central air. The entryway had more floor space than my bedroom, where I walked two steps from bed to dresser to doorway. The living room stretched a million feet out in front of me, with floor-to-ceiling windows wrapping around each side, a view of sloping buildings and looming silvery towers. There was a cream-colored sectional couch with space for ten in front of a gleaming glass coffee table, and a wide dining table past that with clear Lucite chairs neatly tucked around the sides. The last family I had worked for, the Ericksons, had not been this rich. Their apartment in Park Slope was much bigger than mine, but recognizable: it was a place where people lived, a place I could imagine myself into, in some distant future when I had learned to make correct decisions. But this home—the Adriens' home—I would have imagined a literal castle, a gold-walled Versailles, before this real-world counterpart, a living room the size of a basketball court in downtown Manhattan. That you could wake up and eat toast in a place like this.

When I'd spoken to Nathalie on the phone, I'd imagined her imposing and powerful, five foot ten in a pinstriped suit with her hair french-twisted. But in reality, she was around my height, five foot three, and dressed like she was going to spin class: black leggings and a matching white exercise-tank-warm-up-jacket set, her glossy brown hair tied in a low ponytail. I hadn't expected her to be so pretty, with big features—wide blue eyes, full lips—and poreless skin. Her eyebrows made two perfect arches, the kind I could never wrangle mine into. I felt immediately self-conscious, my cheap cardigan trying too hard, the primary colors of my outfit like a kindergarten teacher.

"Come on in," she said, "and please take your shoes off at the door." I crouched down to take off my sandals, fumbling with the buckles. "Did you have any trouble getting here—where do you live again? How long was the commute?"

I answered the questions—Brooklyn, Crown Heights, forty minutes—wondering if this was part of the interview. Was it better if I lived closer? But how could I afford to? She led me to sit on the couch.

"Bijou isn't home from cooking camp. I've spoken to several people on the phone this week, so forgive me if I'm repeating myself, but I'll tell you a bit about her?" I began to agree, but the start of my *yes* dissolved into her next sentence.

"She's about to begin fourth grade. She's so busy and brilliant—ballet, violin, Mandarin, and infatuated with cooking, hence the camp. My husband, Gabe, and I work, as I told you, but I work from home often. Her school is in Soho, two stops away on the 1, and her activities are downtown—Soho or West Village." I thought of what my roommate, Lucy, had said when I asked what she thought the Adriens would be like. "The kind of people who don't ride the subway," she'd said, and I'd nodded, thinking she knew.

"How long have you lived in New York again?" Nathalie asked.

"Almost three years," I said. "And I used to work in the West Village. I'm—comfortable getting around." I hoped she wouldn't ask what my job in the West Village was, and then I'd have to name the sticky bar I'd served picklebacks at.

"So, you've worked for the Ericksons before. I used to work with Marie, years and years ago. She's so lovely. Can you tell me a bit about what that routine was like?"

Lucy used to work for the Ericksons and had sent me in her place one night. I was surprised that they didn't seem to care that I was new. They'd shown me what to microwave for dinner and left me to watch *James and the Giant Peach*. They told me the kids would ask me to lie in their bedroom while they fell asleep in bunk beds, and it felt vaguely illicit, like I should have gone through a background check before watching them slip to sleep. When their parents got home, they gave me eighty dollars for four hours and waved me off cheerily. Lucy eventually relinquished the job to me, and I accepted eagerly—who wouldn't? It was so easy, I could have cried for each morning at the coffee shop when twelve customers in a row told me the boiling water was too hot.

"Sure. They have two kids. So sometimes I'd pick them up from school, or from after-school, and take them home, and . . ." I tried to think of a way to elongate the routine. I'd actually picked them up from school only twice—most of the time I'd shown up at their apartment as their parents headed out the door. "We'd get on the subway from the East

Village, and go back to Park Slope, where they lived, and once home, I'd—fix dinner . . ." I thought of the frozen fish sticks I'd watched spin in the microwave, how I'd squeezed ketchup into a little dish on the counter. "And then I'd help them with their homework, or we'd color—they loved art, coloring books, things like that." She looked at me. "I took them to buy a watercolor set once. And you know, I'd make sure they were in bed by a certain time."

She nodded imperceptibly. What else was I supposed to say?

"Not that we want you to sign a contract, but we do like to have everything set in place once Bijou starts school, so as not to disrupt her routine. Do you have any future plans that would affect how long you could potentially stay with this job? Like graduate school, moving—children of your own?"

I stared at her. People normally thought I was nineteen, even though I was twenty-four. Children of my own? "I'm not planning on any of those, um, anytime soon."

She smiled. "You're young, but you never know! Have you always liked children?"

This was a mistake, I thought. The Ericksons had been so easy, so trusting, I'd imagined that all families were like that, and clearly Nathalie was expecting someone who had prepared, someone who cared, earnestly. I didn't like children; I wanted a job where I didn't have to talk to ninety people per shift who all said the same things. I wanted to stop forcing myself to laugh, I wanted peace. "Yes," I said. "Always. I—I have three siblings. So I grew up with kids around."

A light peeked up from behind her eyes. "Are you the oldest?"

I nodded. "By a lot."

"I'm the same way!" she said. "Three younger siblings. Sometimes I can't believe that I stopped at one of my own, though sometimes it feels like, of course I did."

I opened my mouth and closed it. I was lying, I thought, but then I corrected myself: not really. I did have three younger siblings, even if we weren't from the same family, same house, same two parents.

"It was a lot to manage," I said. "Being the oldest."

She nodded confidentially. I briefly worried she'd ask me for proof of this, as if she'd expect me to have birth certificates. "So many fires to put out." She cast her eyes down for a second. "Sisters, brothers—?"

"Two sisters and a brother," I said. "They're still in school. Two in high school, one in elementary school."

"What a coincidence. I'm the exact same. Two sisters and a brother." There was a flicker I recognized, excitement she felt in this dull connection, that struck me as lonely. How when you felt as if no one had seen you for so long, the slightest bit of kinship felt like intimacy. But I was surprised to see this reaction from her. "*My* baby brother is still in grad school. I do miss it sometimes, the big house." Her phone vibrated on her lap, and she tapped at it with round, shiny nails before turning back to me.

I took a breath in. *I didn't grow up with all my siblings,* I could say, or *They were half siblings, but yes, same, me too.*

"So, obviously, Bijou loves to cook. Loves food. All that. Are you into cooking, yourself? As I said, this will involve some light meal prep."

"Oh, yes, I love food, too," I said carefully, avoiding the active verb. "I have a very small kitchen at my apartment, so it's not the best for cooking. But if I had a bigger kitchen, I would definitely cook more."

"I remember those days," she said. "Well, we have tons of kitchen gadgets here. What would you say is your favorite thing to make?" She noticed my pause. "Back when you had a nice kitchen, of course. Growing up, maybe?"

"Yes, growing up . . ." *Just name a food*, I thought. *Name any food.* "Breakfast was a big deal. Eggs, pancakes." A second passed and I nodded, like I was agreeing with myself.

"So the way we've done this in the past is to bring on a few people part-time for a trial period, and then we can see who meshes the most with Bijou. It ends up being better that way for all involved. Would that work for you?"

I nodded. "I'm still working at the coffee shop at the moment, so I would be fine for a trial period. But I'd like to . . . switch eventually."

"And you're sure this is what you want—full-time?"

The sun shifted and fell in a stripe across her face, so she had to squeeze her eyes shut. "Yes," I said clearly, before they blinked open again. She started to stand up.

"Let me give you a small tour. Gabe will be home with Bijou soon, and you can meet her for a few before I take her to dance, and then you can be on your way."

Was that all? I followed as she walked me through the living room, showing me the kitchen that sat behind french doors. The apartment had an open style, so the living room in the front bled into the dining room in the back, and the kitchen was to the left. "Our bedroom," she said to a set of closed doors past the kitchen, "and my office is back there." She pointed to another shut door on the opposite side of the apartment, next to the entryway. I was having trouble imagining how much space was hidden away behind these doors; how many more rooms were in this apartment? She walked me back toward the elevator, gesturing vaguely down a hallway. "When Bijou was younger, my mom lived with us over in that wing. It's got its own bathroom and a little kitchenette. We think sometimes about having a live-in. Are you open to the possibility of that? We're asking everyone, just in case."

"Live-in?" It was such an intuitive term that after I repeated it, I felt embarrassed. As if I needed her to decipher the English language.

"A live-in nanny. Obviously, that would require further discussion, pay rate and logistics. It might not be relevant, and we may decide against it anyway. But, hypothetically, is that something you'd consider, so we know?"

"Sure, of course," I said. I sounded lukewarm about it, and suddenly I wanted to convince her. "I'm not in love with my apartment, and we're not on a lease." I wanted her to believe me. "It would be really convenient for me, and I wouldn't mind the extra hours."

I wasn't sure why I was saying this, or if I really wanted it. Thinking too far into the future was a problem for me. I loved looking at job listings, internship ideas in careers I'd never dipped a toe in, real estate websites that showed rent I couldn't afford. I wanted to be chosen, or to choose—maybe I wasn't sure of the difference yet. I saw choices glimmering outside my reach, and I wanted badly to get closer.

Nathalie looked at her watch and paused in front of a cluster of pictures on the wall. "Here's Bijou," she said, stroking the top of the portrait. It was a professional photo taken on a beach, a perfect little girl with shoulder-length blonde hair rippling across her face, caught mid-run, her mouth wide in a smile. Next to that one was her school picture, a slim baby-blue headband nestled in her hair, the same smile, with a front tooth missing.

"Gabe and I," Nathalie narrated, pointing to a wedding picture of the two of them, her head on his chest at sunset. She was wearing a strapless white gown with an endless train, her hair gathered intricately at her neck; her husband looked ordinary but adoring. "And here's my siblings and me," and she tapped with her fingernail three times on this one. It was a photo from when they were younger, so I couldn't tell which one Nathalie was. One boy and three girls with tangled limbs, sitting on the top step of a porch, the same eyes and mouths and symmetrical faces. One of the girls stared at the camera and laughed, while the remaining three looked up at her, admiring. I looked closer, trying to pick out which one was Nathalie, but then the elevator rang, and she pulled me away. I fixed a bright smile on my face and turned toward the elevator, waiting to meet the rest of this new family.

2
New York City, 2013

I rubbed my feet restlessly on the Adriens' carpet, pressing my toes into the plush beige fibers so deep that they disappeared. As the afternoon dwindled, the light from their ten-foot windows fell inside honeyed and golden and made me want to fall asleep. I yawned and placed my fingers in a peach ribbon of sun. It was September: autumn only in advertisements, cartoon-orange leaves and red backpacks lining the signs for back-to-school sales, the warmth whittling down but still keeping us in short sleeves. After a month and a half, I'd won out as the full-time nanny, somehow.

Bijou and I were sitting in the entryway. As the most wide-open space, it served as her pseudo-backyard, a place she could twirl in pirouettes, or lie on her stomach drawing, or, today, practice downward-facing dog. At her school, yoga began in the first grade, so it was her fourth year of practice. She was concerned that I did not know as much about vinyasa as she did. She asked if I could do a split, and I couldn't, not anymore—not since I was young, like her, when I wore black leotards in my middle school's basement a dozen years ago.

"Can you?" she asked again. I shook my head, and Bijou slid her legs on either side of her body to show me that she could. She was still in her school skirt, a pleated navy blue with the Stanton Academy crest sewn in yellow thread above the right knee, and I noticed she was starting to sprout leg hair. It was so blonde it wasn't visible as much as reflective, shimmering with the last wisps of sun. She popped up and went back to downward dog.

"What did you play in school when you were a kid?" She kicked her right leg into the air, away from her tented body, and then brought it in front of her torso, bending it into a neat ninety-degree angle while her left leg lay straight. "This is called pigeon."

"Softball." I lay on my side, stretching my arms toward the exit. "Kickball."

"What's kickball?" She held her arms out stick-straight, like a zombie, and then collapsed forward over her leg. Her school called gym class "cooperative teamwork time."

I was debating whether to explain kickball when we heard the rumble of the elevator doors. I still felt special about being in an apartment that had an elevator open right into the living room. When I'd told Lucy about it, she'd marveled, "Wow. Imagine being so rich, you're actually *unable* to lose your keys?" Lucy had locked herself out of our apartment twice that month alone.

I scrambled to sit up and look alert before Nathalie came in. When the doors opened, it was her husband, Gabriel, and I slouched back down. He wasn't home as much, and even though I'd been in his home for almost two months, I didn't know what to call him. Mr. Adrien sounded too formal, Gabe seemed too casual, and I'd never heard anyone actually say Gabriel. He was a doctor, and tonight he'd left his white lab coat on, sticking out from under the hem of his jacket. He looked at us sitting on the floor as the doors slid shut behind him, and his voice was tentative as it came out.

"Hello, you two," he said. He didn't know how to talk to me either.

"I've been showing Willa how to do yoga," Bijou said, standing up in front of me. "She didn't even know what pigeon was!" The end of her french braid was right in front of my face. I thought about tugging it and then I did. She whipped her head around, confused.

"Sorry." Guilt pinpricked my chest. "A strand was loose." I rearranged the bracelets on my wrist. "Um, have you heard from Nathalie? She hasn't told me what to do about dinner."

Gabe's eyes widened a bit, and he shook his head, turning toward the coat closet. "No, I haven't." He removed his jacket and then his lab coat, hanging each of them up before shutting the door. When he turned back around, he looked surprised to see me still looking at him. "I'm sure there's something in the fridge?"

"I'll go look," I said. I hadn't thought the light meal prep would be so complicated, that there were no frozen fish sticks in this house. There were only meals made from scratch and my constant fear of infecting Bijou with something like salmonella.

"I'll come," Bijou chirped, skipping until she was in line with me. Taking care of a child meant being under constant scrutiny, no escape for even two minutes into the kitchen by myself. I opened the fridge hopefully; I still hadn't cooked without meticulous instructions from Nathalie. Bijou had the palate of a classically trained chef. She often asked me to buy langoustines or duck liver when I went to the grocery store, and spent her allotted television time on competitive cooking shows. Each time I put a plate in front of her, I thought she might take one bite and give me a rundown of its flaws. Sometimes, she did.

Bijou was nine and a half, but not the way I was once nine and a half. *How many languages do you speak? What instruments do you play? How many countries have you been to? Can you do a split?* I rubbed my temples whenever she started on the litany of questions that seemed so popular among the widely trained. *None, nothing, no.*

"Here's some chicken," I said, fishing out some fleshy pink pieces wrapped in plastic.

"Oh, these shallots are old," Bijou said, standing on her tiptoes to look through a bowl of produce.

I still wasn't exactly sure what shallots were. Something like garlic? "Okay. There's some tomato sauce. I can make you pasta with tomato sauce and chicken? Like chicken parm." I tried to sound confident. Kids were supposed to take what you said at face value—I'd heard that somewhere.

"But do we have mozzarella for that?"

Is that what's in chicken parm? "Why don't you go talk to your dad?" I said. "Ask him how his day was. See if he wants chicken parm." I took a large skillet under her gaze and switched the flame on underneath. Their stove's brushed steel was so smooth and easy, a bright blue flame with the slightest flick of my wrist. I drizzled olive oil in the pan and looked at her, thinking, *See? I know what I'm doing.*

She shrugged and scampered out. I searched *easy chicken parm* on my phone, then filled up a large pot with water. I could see my reflection in their stainless-steel pots, my face bent like an hourglass, a funhouse image of my tan skin, my black hair, my nervous brown eyes staring back at me. I unwrapped the chicken breasts and flinched at how slimy and wet they felt between my fingers. I dropped two in the pan and immediately felt the hot spatter of oil on my wrists. I jerked away quickly, rubbing at my arm.

"Are you okay?" Bijou said as she walked back in. I nodded and dropped my hands to my sides.

"If you *place* it in gently, it seems like it will splatter but it won't," Bijou said crisply.

"What?" I said, dropping another piece the same way. She yelped as if burned. "Oops, sorry." I turned the faucet on and pulled her toward it. "Did that really get you?"

"Did you salt the water?" Bijou asked, pointing her chin at the stove.

"I was about to," I said, and left her with her wrist outstretched under the cold water. As I grabbed the salt, I saw Gabe in the doorway. He cleared his throat. Bijou turned off the faucet and came to stand by my side. She was so tall for her age, almost at my shoulders, and I could feel her elbow against mine as we looked up at him.

"Nathalie's over at Amico—she said she'll bring us something to eat from there. Sorry you already started, Willa. She said that she meant to tell you."

"Ooh." Bijou reached behind me to turn off the stove. "I love the duck there."

I looked at the burners. "Should I finish that and put it away, or . . . ?" The chicken breasts were still half flesh and half meat, like pulsing organs on a pan.

"I hate to say it, but you better throw it out. We have dinner plans tomorrow and then we're away this weekend. Thanks, Willa. They were about to go bad anyway."

I tipped the pan into the garbage and covered the mess up with paper towels. One, two, three chicken breasts, cage-free and organic. They could have fed me for a week. I shouldn't have asked Gabe—Nathalie would have told me something different. Most times while we fixed dinner, Bijou talked about how good Nathalie was at making this, how Nathalie's mother had taught her that.

"Did your parents cook much?" Nathalie had asked me once when I'd left the lid on a pot of boiling water, and it overflowed onto the stove. She'd been in a good mood that day and had said it playfully, not like the time I didn't put enough bread crumbs in the meatballs and she'd raised her eyebrows at their soggy shapes.

"My mom worked," I'd said with my back turned, crumpling a paper towel into the trash. Nathalie murmured something tactfully, and we avoided what was in front of us on the counter: evidence of Nathalie's own career, stacks of folders and files and notes that she'd been working on before she'd seen the lid trembling.

3

New York City, 2013

Mondays were dance. Ballet in the spring, tap in the fall, with recital costumes as elaborate as wedding gowns, silk, tulle, satin, mini-crystals hanging off the straps. Tuesdays were violin, taken in the music room upstairs at school, so she could walk up after class on her own, and I didn't have to be in Tribeca until four thirty. Wednesdays were her free day, spent on homework or cultural activities. We'd take the subway to the Met or paint ceramic bowls or walk the perimeter of a park with flash cards and hot apple cider. Thursdays she had Mandarin, private lessons out of a West Village brownstone with a woman named Li. I felt like Li distrusted me immediately because I was one of those American-born Chinese kids who wasn't really Chinese enough. I was used to it, but each Thursday I still hoped Nathalie might cancel on me; I still caressed the idea of calling out sick.

On Fridays, there were no activities. Her parents would sometimes come home from work early on the start of the weekend, to eat dinner together or watch a movie or . . . I don't know. Whatever families did.

*

To pick Bijou up for dance class, I had to collect her from her classroom, and she'd make me take the stairs down seven flights for "exercise" before we headed to the subway. On days she wanted to annoy me, she'd slide under the turnstile and look up at me, waiting to be yelled at. Bijou told me that it was okay for her to do this, even as she had a student MetroCard in her pocket. The first time she'd done it, I'd playfully pushed at her back, but secretly I was terrified that she'd broken some kind of law and I'd be forced to say to a police officer, "I don't know, I'm not really in charge of this dynamic here."

I sat on an empty bench and took out a book I'd been carrying around. A small girl jumped up on the bench next to me and I inched away. How had I ended up here? I tried to smile at the little girl as I got up and went over to the windows of Bijou's class. She liked it when I came up in the middle of class and waved, even though I thought it must annoy the teacher. I couldn't parse if it was a childlike desire or an urge to check up on me, to make sure I wasn't acting too off-the-clock. I stood and watched the young girls swivel and twirl in their black leotards and pink tights. Bijou waved at me sloppily, like she was excited and forgot her manners. I waved back and rejoined the room of still, expectant bodies. This was what money bought—someone waiting for you, right outside the door.

I put my book back into my purse. I didn't want to read. Someone had left a West Elm catalog on the bench, and what I wanted was a bed frame. I'd lived in New York for almost three amorphous years in two rented rooms. The first room already had a bed frame when I got there, a giant wooden sleigh bed that the previous tenant had left. No one could manage to lift it, and I didn't have a bed frame, so I kept it.

When I moved out, I left it there too. I'd been in my new apartment for almost nine months, and I kept thinking I'd buy one soon. But we lived in a fourth-floor walk-up, and packages were always getting stolen. I couldn't imagine the disaster of accepting a bed frame. I paged through the quirky names of headboards, all their rounded shapes, and picked out which I'd take if I had the space, the money, the drive to actually follow through. Then I tossed them back on the bench.

A text came in from Nathalie. *You can make a quick shrimp scampi tonight. Shrimp in freezer. Everything else at home, but might need more garlic. Remember: shrimp cooks quickly! No more than 2–3 minutes per side.*

I'd made shrimp tacos, or attempted to, for Bijou the other day. I'd been nervous about how pale and gray they were until they became stiff curls of white and pink. "This is like rubber," Bijou said, tearing the tail off one with her teeth. "These were *nice shrimp.*" It was true they'd come from a fancy seafood market nearby, cold and slimy in a plastic bag. I told her to put more salsa on top but felt uneasy after she invoked the price. I hadn't realized she'd told Nathalie. When Bijou came out, I tossed her bag at her. "Let's go," I said shortly. "We need to buy garlic."

*

I never imagined that someone who worked for a bank could work from home as often as Nathalie did. She walked around the apartment in monochromatic exercise clothes or silky-looking loungewear, video-chatting into business meetings. I didn't always know when she was home, either.

Her office was off to the side of the living room, the door shut, and I was never sure if we were alone.

One day, she'd called to me from her office. Bijou and I were in the kitchen, doing her homework. She was tracing Chinese characters, and I was watching her make the strokes. I'd known Nathalie was home because she'd greeted us in black leggings and a soft-looking striped sweater. She looked young when she wasn't dressed up, and I realized that she couldn't be past her midthirties, maybe twelve years older than I was. But around her, I felt like a sixth grader in the home of the senior prom queen, finally invited into her lair.

"I'm trying to declutter," Nathalie said when I walked in. Everything in her office was pastel and precise, a sharp-lined desk, a pale pink rug, silver-framed photos on the wall of her, Bijou, and Gabe. I looked up at the pictures, one of Bijou and Nathalie, leaning their heads toward each other. Nathalie sat on a velvet sofa, holding a box on her lap.

"You know when you order a hundred dollars of something and they send you these samples? I keep them, but I realized I need to purge." There was a glass-on-glass clatter as she held the box upside down, and a stream of jars spilled out onto the table. "There," she said. "So many! I wanted to see if you wanted any before I threw them out?"

"Samples?" I said, holding up a full-sized bottle of moisturizer in a frosted-glass jar.

"Oh, I guess some of them are old products I never used. But I'm so set in my ways now, I can't stray." She got up from the couch and sat in her computer chair. "If you're the same way, you don't have to take any. Do you have a skincare routine?"

"Not really." I bent to sort through the jars. They were like little pieces of jewelry, a clear pink case of eye cream, a jagged-shaped clear bottle of moisturizer, little liquid bottles with delicate script.

"You have such nice skin, though. You're not Korean, are you?"

"I'm half Chinese." Didn't she remember my last name was Chen?

"I love Korean skin-care," she said. "It's totally changed my skin. I wish I'd started even earlier. They say that in Korea, the girls start doing this routine at fifteen."

"Oh, really?" I felt that this blank phrase was what I said the most around Nathalie, never sure of how to respond.

"Was your mom into skin care?"

"Oh, no, my mom's never really been into the beauty thing." I hesitated, wondering if I should tell Nathalie that my mom was white. I glanced at her, and she was looking at me attentively. I looked back to the bottles, nervous.

"My mom was so controlling with that stuff when I was younger," Nathalie said. "I had to wear my hair or dress the way she wanted. And she wouldn't let me wear makeup until I was fifteen or so. I felt like that was the hardest thing in the world."

"I guess when you're young, you want to be older," I said, commending myself for the full sentence.

"Yes, believe me, *enjoy* being young," she said. "Enjoy not having to have a skin-care routine, because if I don't put night creams on, you can tell."

Maybe Nathalie did think I was a few years younger than I was, just out of college, even though she'd asked me about having kids. Maybe she thought I was young enough that I didn't have to think about starting my life or fending off wrinkles. But anyone could tell that her skin looked more like glass than mine. I smiled politely at her comment. "Are there any that you recommend?" I was still kneeling on the floor in front of the table, not sure how many I could take. There must have been thirty. "How many do I need?"

"Oh, honestly you could take them all. But here, let's see." She bent next to me. I noticed that she had a bland little star tattoo on the inside of her wrist. She gathered up eight or nine, pushed them toward me. "How about these?"

I thanked her and she handed me a little shopping bag folded up near her desk. I placed the bottles in, hearing them *clink, clink, clink* against each other. "Thanks so much," I said again. "I'm excited to try them." I felt like I had to keep telling her.

"Not that you *need* anything. Such pretty skin," she said. "It's so great that your mom didn't push you into a beauty routine."

I nodded but felt like I was lying. I wondered again if I should tell her my mom was not Asian like I was, to see if that changed things, but it felt too uncomfortable, presumptuous somehow, like it would change the pleasant, generous energy filling the room. So I smiled, and said nothing.

4

New York City, 2013

I heard Nathalie talking to someone on speakerphone when we walked into the apartment one Friday. Bijou told me they were making paella that evening, and I had hoped Nathalie would be home early, so she could take over rather than me. I noticed the air was citrusy with cleaning products as Nathalie leaned out of the kitchen and waved for us to come in. Bijou slid in her socks toward her. I hovered by the doorframe.

When Nathalie hung up, she reached over to kiss Bijou on the forehead and, with one hand still on her phone, turned on a playlist. I expected something soft or sweet, but the opening bars of "Miss You" by the Rolling Stones came on. Nathalie had laid everything out in neat piles on the counter, the way Bijou sometimes did, as if performing a demo: little bowls of veiny gray shrimp and slippery red chorizo and knives resting on cutting boards, waiting for the cooks to take their stations.

"Should I—did you want me to go?" I asked.

"I think we need all hands on deck, right, Bee?"

Bijou nodded, shyly, looking at the counter. If she had been looking at me, I would have looked down, too, but since she wasn't, I took a moment to linger on her cheek as I took in her nod, how powdery-soft her skin was, and the way her eyelashes caught the light as they fluttered. I smiled at the side of her face, knowing she wouldn't see, and then I asked Nathalie what I should do.

"Why don't *you*," Nathalie said, "start chopping this parsley? Very fine, but it doesn't have to be neat."

I tried to concentrate on the task as much as Bijou was on crushing her garlic cloves. She had her own set of kitchen knives with pink rubber handles, though she was only allowed to use them when Nathalie was home. She laid the flat edge of the knife over each clove carefully, placing it in the perfect spot, and then leaned on it with her hands, her whole body forward as if about to leap. The clove would pop, and she'd take back the knife and study it before moving on. We stood next to each other on the far side of the kitchen island, each of us before a cutting board. Nathalie was across from us, trimming the fat from chicken breasts using a pair of scissors, humming to herself as her hands wove around each other.

When I finished the parsley, one pan was hissing with chicken and the other with chorizo. Into an empty pot, Nathalie dropped the onions she'd chopped, the garlic Bijou had crushed, and the parsley I'd mangled, and she poured a can of tomato puree on top, drizzling the red sauce in a circle. She stood in front of the stove while Bijou and I stayed on the other side of the kitchen island. Her face was bare and pink from the steam in a way that made her look young and clean.

"This is called sofrito," she said. "It's a sauce you use as a base."

I stood next to Bijou, my right foot almost touching her left, and I thought about how this scene would appear if painted or peered in upon. I suspended for a moment the reality of how I looked, which I often did if there were no mirrors around. I saw only what I could see, my hands on the counter next to Bijou's, my feet barely bigger than hers, the identically painted toenails we'd done days before. We rested our hands on the marble, leaning forward slightly. Nathalie was on the other side, praising our craftsmanship at elemental tasks in the way that parents ought to do. We stood there at attention, nodding at her praise. We stood there like sisters, maybe. If someone had looked in the window and seen the backs of our heads, would they have known any different? Out of the corner of my eye, I saw Bijou's cheeks flush pink, as mine must have, rosy from the warmth of Nathalie's attention. I felt a hot kind of jealousy for how Bijou would turn out, having been raised in the arms of someone who knew what she was doing. For how she woke up in the lemon glow of Nathalie's attention. It was more luck than I could bear, and here I was, being paid to stand by and hold watch.

5

Durland, New Jersey, 2004

I was fourteen and it was Tuesday night at Jack's Asian Delicacies. Fried banana ice cream was two dollars, pot stickers were three, and my mom had guilted me into coming here with her and her husband for discount Asian food.

A red-haired waiter walked over to tell us the specials. "The last one is baby tako," he said, pronouncing it *tay-koh.* "It's baby octopus, five pieces, six ninety-five."

"It's actually *tah-koh,*" Ray said after he left. "They had it a few weeks ago. I was going to tell him, but that's not my job."

I knew that, too, but didn't say it. My dad had ordered them for us before. I didn't want Ray to know that I liked them. "Did you know octopuses have nine brains?" I said instead, more to my mom.

"Sure I did," he said from the other side of her.

"Really," I said, taking my chopsticks from their paper sleeve and breaking them apart. "You knew that?"

"That's why I like them," he said. "I eat them and get smarter with each meal."

"It probably means we *shouldn't* eat them."

"No one is making you," he said, and I quieted down because I did want to eat them, even if they had nine brains.

I liked their firm-soft texture and blackened tentacles, their egg-shaped heads without crunchy skulls. But at least I wanted to eat them despite their nine brains, not because of them.

"Where'd you learn that, Willa? In school today?" my mom asked.

"Um, no." I felt like she was three beats slower than the conversation, asking about things only when I was over talking about them, missing whatever subtext simmered beneath the sentences. She looked at me, and my eye sockets twinged. "We're reading *A Separate Peace*," I added in an attempt to be nice, prying the words from the back of my throat.

"By the way, what time did you get in last night?" she said to Ray. My mom was a nurse and worked night shifts a lot. Ray was a security guard, so sometimes he did too. I didn't sleep well, so I often knew exactly when Ray came home from the thump of his unlaced boots, the heave of the fridge door, the clatter of his final beer bottle into the recycling. My mom should've asked me.

She'd started seeing him when I was at the tail end of middle school. I'd never thought of her as lonely, or romantic, or dateable: she was my parent. But suddenly, she was red-lipped and stinging my eyes with perfume, all high-pitched laughter and quiet nods, buying gauzy, lacy clothes and washing her hair all the time. She was cleaning corners of the house we'd let pile up and lighting candles on the dinner table. She thought I needed to get out more. It seemed like an eternity since it had been just my mom and me.

We were sitting at the sushi bar, in front of the lone Asian employee, who wore a scarf folded over his forehead and bowed when presenting dishes. I put my chin in my hand and picked up my chopsticks, tapped them lightly on the plate. Our server dropped off crab rangoon and a beer. My mom was on call, so she drank water. It was rare for them to go to a restaurant and rarer for them to bring me. I didn't know why my mom had insisted I come. We used to go out every so often for tacos or Italian food, but Ray only liked this place, Jack's Asian Delicacies. There weren't many culture-specific Asian restaurants near us, nothing exclusively Thai or Korean or Japanese. There were only restaurants that served all of the above, sushi and kimchi and sesame chicken, and called themselves Asian. Ray was white like boiled potatoes cut into quarters, white like flour that sticks to skin, but he was also obsessed with pad thai and sweet-and-sour soup, and his hair was like mine—close enough to black that everyone called it that. That was one reason I didn't like him; when I was with him and my mom, people assumed I was his before being told I was hers.

Secretly, I loved Jack's too. At school, everything that touched my lips was preplanned to make me dissolve into the background. I ate the pizza we got on Fridays with red sugared sauce, potato chips from the vending machine that shredded the roof of my mouth, and cold wraps with chicken and cheese and lettuce that was more air than leaf. I wouldn't be caught dead with something that needed soy sauce.

Once, I'd been asked if I bathed in it, and since that day I'd made sure to eat the plainest food available, whatever everyone else was eating. I couldn't have been less remarkable, couldn't have called for less attention, but still, that kind always came—from kids at school, from teachers, from parents, from strangers. They told me how my eyes looked like almonds or how my skin was olive, which never made sense to me. Weren't olives black or green? They compared me to something sweet—caramel, honey, butterscotch—and after a while I felt like them: sticky. It made me hold on to my arms tightly, protectively, when I was in public, because sometimes as they contemplated me, they ran a finger across my skin, as if they could swipe up some of the taste. As if they were testing out the texture—how would it feel to take a scoop? It was enough to turn me off sweetness forever.

*

"Baby tay-koh," our waiter mispronounced grandly, placing down a plate of five.

"Are you going to try, Willa?" my mom asked. When I was young, before I noticed I was different, I used to ask for egg-drop soup and fried rice and even anchovies. She never noticed that I thought so much about what I could eat in public, what I could bring to school, how I asked her to buy the kind of bread you could mold between your hands and cheese that was individually wrapped in plastic. But how could she understand? Her blonde hair fell out of her ponytail in wisps, and behind glasses sat her chlorine-pool eyes. If I looked like her, I wouldn't understand either.

"Yup," I said. I picked one of them up and thought about biting off a few of his tentacles, curled lifelessly around the little blob of a head. Instead, I pushed the entire thing in my mouth and chewed.

My mom ate one and told us we could have the rest. Ray speared another one immediately, and I pulled the plate back to my side—there was only one left. I placed it directly in front of me while I chewed my first one slowly. They were so much softer than you might think: squishy, forgiving, the little ribbing on their tentacles fitting snugly against the top of my mouth. *Nine brains and three hearts.* I'd read it in a book at the library. Imagine having three hearts? Nine brains? I imagined my brain count growing like in a video game each time one passed down my throat.

My mom turned as someone behind us said her name.

"Sophie!" It was Ashley Finnegan and her mom, who volunteered at the hospital my mom worked at. My mom didn't have a lot of friends, said she didn't fit in with the moms here. As I watched them greet each other, I realized that there was something that set her apart, but I didn't know what it was.

Ashley was in my grade. She had strawberry-blonde hair that dried straight as a sheet even when she came to school with it wet; she could coil it on top of her head for gym class, and it would still be a glossy wave once she let it down. She was one of five girls named Ashley, all best friends, who often wore the same outfits in different colors like a girl band.

"Ashley," her mom prompted in a loud whisper, pushing her my way. I squirmed in my seat. Here with my mom and my stepdad, without the armor of my few friends, I felt exposed, like a nerve sticking out from skin.

"Hey, Willa," she said. "What's up?"

I twisted my body so that I was facing her. "Nothing, really."

"What *is* that?" she said, bending forward to look at my plate, her hair brushing past my shoulder with a whoosh of vanilla-cupcake fumes. I turned my head back toward the baby tako and looked, as if I didn't know. There was one left, alone in a puddle of dark-blemished grease, a spotlight shining on the reddish tinge to its skin, the underside of bumpy tentacles.

"It looks like a grilled alien," Ashley said.

I could see what she meant. "It's baby octopus."

"*Baby* octopus?" she repeated. I nodded. She backed a couple of inches away. "That's sick," she said, her face scrunched as the hair tie around her wrist.

"You never had octopus before?" Ray said.

Ashley straightened. "No, is that, like, a normal thing to eat?" She twirled her frosting-scented hair around a finger and gave a small laugh.

"Oh, well, it's not *ordinary.*" He leaned into the gap our mothers made while they talked. "But yeah, it's like a special delicacy. It tastes like chicken, like a chewy chicken."

She pushed her pink-glossed lips together in consideration, and then her mom motioned for them to leave, and she looked back at the plate. She left quickly, a short wave.

Ray turned back around and held up his beer. My mom turned to him, said, "Are you sure you should—?" There was a loud crunch of crab rangoon. He'd forgotten our conversation already. My ears thrummed with the way that Ashley said *baby*, the way she backed away. I knew Ray hadn't answered her to save me, but only because he couldn't fathom embarrassment. He would have spoken that proudly about anything. It wasn't like the people in my town hadn't heard of Asian food, but they talked about most of it like it was dirty and drenched in some kind of guilt. Sometimes the

Ashleys brought in sushi for lunch, blocky California rolls they soaked with soy sauce. But they were allowed to. They couldn't be traced back to it.

"Remember when you and Ashley were in the play in sixth grade?" my mom said. It had been *Annie.* I thought there was no one else in my town who understood a girl desperate for two parents the way I did, but the red wig matched Ashley, her freckles, her eyes. "Do you ever see her anymore?"

I shook my head but didn't elaborate. My mom cleared her throat, and when I looked up, she said, "We have some news."

Her two hands, on her stomach in a V. I thought of how the three of them would look in a photo together, of how I'd look with them. I took a chopstick and speared the little octopus through its fleshy head. I held it up like that, on a spoke, and rotated it in front of my face. Octopuses don't have any bones; they can squeeze through spaces as small as cracks. I pushed it into my mouth. No one could possibly want another heart. But imagine being boneless, able to pinch yourself so small no one could find you.

6

New York City, 2013

It was October, and the quilted leaves crunching underfoot reminded me of routines and schedules, alarm clocks and coffee. I showed up on time to work each day, feeling eager to please. Sometimes I arrived at the apartment early, and the doorman would send me upstairs to wait. The apartment was spotless and empty at that time; the housekeeper, Donna, came in the mornings. I'd circle the long sectional couch in the middle of the room or walk along the walls looking at the framed photos—a few shots of Nathalie and Gabe, but mostly it was Bijou: newborn Bijou in Nathalie's arms, Bijou as a toddler next to a pile of leaves, Bijou onstage at a recital, Bijou and Gabe at a baseball game.

After a few minutes of restless motion, I'd slink to the cushioned bench below the windows, curl my legs under me, and lean my forehead against the cool glass. I tried to stay upright so that if they surprised me, I wouldn't look too relaxed. They lived on a quiet street, so it wasn't all taxicabs and traffic and bike messengers. I saw servers arriving for their shifts at the restaurant across the street, pulling neckties out of their pockets or finishing their cigarettes while talking on the phone. I watched people walking with shiny shopping bags, women with linked arms or couples with intertwined hands. They stopped for cappuccinos and muffins at the bakery diagonal from the building, with its pastel yellow awning and rickety chairs out front. Sometimes there would be tourists taking pictures on the cobblestone. I wondered if anyone looked up and saw me, my forehead leaning against the glass. If anyone from above ever noticed me when I was down below. Whenever the elevator opened, that was my clock-in, like any other job, time to be corrected, quietly judged. Very watched, which wasn't the same as being seen.

*

I looked around the kitchen and tried to lay out the ingredients Bijou had mentioned before. There was the imported pasta that came in green boxes with yellow type, stacked in a tall row in their cabinet. Nitrate-free bacon and free-range eggs, a wedge of parmesan we'd have to grate. A picture hung in Bijou's room that she'd made for career day, curlicue letters next to a whisk, spelling out *I want to be a chef when I grow up, because I love cooking with my family.* I had cycled through stages of desire with so many occupations—actress, doctor, teacher, therapist—but I had never, never wanted to be a chef.

"Okay," Bijou said as she walked in, her voice serious. "So usually we divide the tasks. Mom lets me chop when she's home, but you have to do it since she's not here. And she always cooks the bacon, because of the oil."

I leaned my elbows on the counter and looked at her.

"Because it could hurt me," she elaborated.

"Ah. So I'll do that."

She nodded. "We'll start boiling water for the pasta and grating the cheese. And then I'll make the sauce, but I have to wait until just before it's ready."

I put my hand to my forehead and saluted her. She stood on the other side of the island as I cooked the bacon, handed me the knives by their handles and backed away. Each time we made dinner without Nathalie we went through this routine; what she was and wasn't allowed to do if Nathalie wasn't home. I was, I don't know, touched? By how much she wanted to obey her mom. It wasn't that Bijou was generally obedient, because she questioned things constantly, but when it came to Nathalie, she wouldn't chop a stem of celery unless she was allowed. Was she sure that she would be caught if she disobeyed, or did she believe each word Nathalie said? Both answers—how monitored she felt, how easily she trusted—seemed right. Through the wide kitchen windows, I could see into a couple of apartments across the way. I imagined that to them I looked like a cloudy-edged stunt double, someone stepping in to take on the dangerous acts, as Bijou flitted around the kitchen, independently preparing Italian cuisine.

*

"There's always someone with more," my mom used to say. I had a small imagination, I realized. I had thought that the Adriens were rich-rich. But as I took Bijou around Lower Manhattan on playdates, I saw that she must feel like what she had was average. I took her to penthouse apartments where one staff member took our coats and another brought us lemon water. I took her to brownstones in the West Village that were bigger than the house I grew up in, with grand pianos in the entryway and screening rooms in the basement. She had friends whose bedroom windows looked out onto the Freedom Tower past their piles of toys; whose apartments had wraparound balconies with fire pits and padded couches; friends who had Japanese toilets with heated seats, personal chefs to make them eggs in the morning, rooftops with swimming pools, room in their foyers for conceptual sculptures. And they all had nannies, most of whom lived with them. Some of the nannies were serious and read books on child psychology, and some of them were younger and more carefree. One offered me wine in a coffee cup while we watched the two kids do cartwheels, telling me that the dad never checked his wine cellar. I drank it happily, and on the walk home asked Bijou when we could go back.

Skylar lived in the building with the pool, which I only found out about after pool weather had ended. I wished for the summer, imagined reading a book half in the water while they did headstands in the shallow end. But for now, we sat inside Skylar's gigantic playroom while they watched music videos. Her nanny was older, motherly, and I felt shy around her. She offered me different kinds of tea and poured in cream and put out a basket of gingersnaps. Bijou and Skylar were singing along loudly, trying to replicate the dances. I took out a book and stared at the white space in the margins.

"Bee," I called when it was almost five. "Mandarin starts soon."

She pouted but stopped shimmying. "Can we walk there?" she asked.

Nathalie told me her Mandarin teacher's name was Lixin Zhang. Bijou told me it was actually Zhang Lixin and the right way to address her was Zhang Lǎoshī, which meant Teacher Zhang, but that she let the students call her Li. I didn't feel allowed to be on a first-name basis with her, but I also didn't feel like I could correctly pronounce the word *lǎoshī,* and if I said it wrong, it was more embarrassing than if Nathalie or Gabe did, so the few times I'd said hello, I'd said Mrs. Zhang, something no one had told me to say.

"Hi," I said and cut myself off to simply wave as she ushered Bijou inside and shut the door. I turned away. The irony was not lost on me as I dropped Bijou off to learn my father's first language and sat waiting outside. I sank cross-legged to the carpet, put the same book next to my legs, and picked up my phone. I thought about texting my dad. We only ever communicated via text, every month or so, sometimes more, sometimes less. I tried not to think of him too much. But, lately, life felt like a permanent state of sitting outside doors, thinking of things I didn't want to, while Bijou got better at things I'd never know.

"Willa?" I looked up. It was Gabe. I quickly untangled my legs and stood. I was dressed like a college student; jeans ripped over my thighs, a striped T-shirt under a zip-up hoodie under a leather jacket. In the beginning I'd erred on the side of formality, aiming for what I thought was a presentable yet casual dress code, but I'd never had a job where I couldn't wear tank tops or jeans. It took me a couple of weeks to boomerang back to dressing like a kid.

"Hi," I said. "Are you picking Bijou up?"

"Oh, God," he said. "I was supposed to text you and tell you. I got caught up and—"

"Oh, it's okay." I looked at my watch. "She'll be done in ten minutes."

"Do you sit out here the whole time? She should put a chair out here," he said.

It had never occurred to me, that this situation should be made more comfortable. I blushed, like it was a failing of mine. "Well, sometimes I go get a coffee next door, but—" I paused. I had been about to say, *Bijou likes it when you wait for her*, but didn't want to tell him what his own daughter's preferences were.

"I actually have the car with me today, so I can drive her home. If you want to wait, I could take you to the subway?"

"Oh, that's okay, I can walk," I said. I picked my purse off the floor and put the strap on my shoulder. "Oh . . ." My voice trailed off. "I forgot I left some stuff at your apartment. I'll stop by on my way."

"And walk all that way? I can drive you home with us when she's done."

I didn't want to be impolite, but I would have rather left.

He glanced at the floor quickly. "So there's a coffee shop nearby? Should we sit there for a few minutes? She's not done until six, right?"

"Yeah, six," I said. "Sure."

"Lead the way."

We walked out of the building and over to the coffee shop next door. The tabletops were rough slabs of marble, and there were six types of drip coffee. Gabe walked a few paces away from me with his hands deep in his coat pockets. He had broad shoulders that made a box out of his navy-blue peacoat and sandy-blond hair that curled at the ends. His cheeks raised into two nubby circles when he smiled, in a way that seemed childlike. I couldn't think of one thing to say to him. I imagined he was regretting this idea as well.

I ordered a plain coffee and Gabe asked for an Americano. The barista asked if we were together. I stood there as Gabe nodded and reached for his wallet, wondering if I should have offered to pay for my own. We sat at one of the tables near the front, and I squinted at the clock on the wall. We still had six minutes.

"Bijou's getting really good at Chinese, I think," I said. "It's pretty cool."

"Isn't it?" he said. "She's picking it up fast. I'm so impressed with her."

"Me too," I said quietly. I ran my fingers around the sleeve of my coffee cup, raised it to my mouth.

"She's such a studious girl too. I don't know about you, but I wasn't as enthused about doing homework at her age. Were you?"

I laughed. "No," I said. "Not at all." I tried to think of a way to elaborate that wasn't truthful enough to make him regret hiring me.

He said, "Are you in school?" as I said, "Where did you grow up?" We froze for a second in an awkward smile.

"I finished school," I said. "A, um, a couple years ago. I was studying psychology."

The question of what I was doing next seemed to hang in the air, and he tried another tactic.

"And you worked for Marie before?"

"Yeah, but that was part-time, so she referred me to Nathalie when she was looking for someone new. When your old nanny left?"

"Right, Jessica went to get her doctorate in Kansas. Or Kentucky, I can't remember."

I wanted to ask Gabe something, but I had nothing to go on, nothing I'd wondered about him. I didn't know if he was a surgeon or an anesthesiologist or worked in the ER. I knew the intimate details of their lives, but none of the more routine ones. I took a sip of my coffee and thought of what else I could say. I had forgotten to add milk.

"My roommate, Lucy—she and I used to work at a coffee shop together in Crown Heights, but she also babysat on the side. I used to work at two different coffee shops, but she convinced me to switch all my shifts to this one, but then she left, so . . ." I swallowed. I had meant this to sound light, but I heard myself speaking as if I had been abandoned. "So she suggested me to the Ericksons for babysitting because I wasn't loving the coffee shop anymore. Management switch—we all hated the new owners."

"Ah, I see," he said. I could tell he was trying but couldn't remember, or didn't know, problems like these. "But you two still live together?"

"Kind of," I said with a slight laugh. "She has this boyfriend. She's always at his place. I have it to myself a lot."

"Are you from nearby? Where do your parents live?" he asked.

"I grew up in New Jersey," I said. "My dad lives upstate. My mom in New Jersey. So, both close."

"Do you get to see them often?"

"No," I said before I could edit. "I don't see them much. They're not really—they have other families." I hadn't meant to say that, but I was jumpy with nerves. The door opened next to us, and a gust of wind blew my napkin off the table. "Where are you from?" I asked back. It came out of my mouth unnaturally, and I realized I never asked those words. I was asked them far too much, in far too aggressive a tone. But to someone like Gabe, they meant nothing.

"My hometown—" He reached for the napkin, which he crumpled in his fist. "Entirely different story from here. I'm from way upstate in New York, in the Adirondacks, altitude so high it's above the tick line. The nearest school was miles away, and it was a hundred and twenty kids from pre-K to grade twelve."

"Wow. I thought I went to a small school," I said. "I had a hundred kids in my class."

"I had four for years, and then this miracle happened—twins my age moved in. Fifty percent increase. Sometimes Bee complains her class is small. I always say that to her." He smiled a little to himself, growing the fat cherries of his cheeks. He checked his watch. "Is it time?"

I could see it in him, the small-town-ness. How for him it must have been comforting instead of suffocating. Maybe if everyone looked like you, you wouldn't spend the whole time counting, outnumbered. I nodded and picked up my coffee. "Yup," I said brightly. "Let's go." As we walked out, I said stiffly, "Thank you for the coffee." I felt as if he were babysitting me.

*

At home that night, I stuck two pieces of bread in the toaster. Nathalie had given me a loaf of homemade bread that week, made for her by a friend. She was trying to go gluten-free, she'd explained. I spread butter on one of the slices. It tasted nutty and dense, too healthy, but I kept eating it. Their castoffs were irresistible to me. Nathalie would make piles of clothes to give away inside her walk-in closet and, before having them picked up for Goodwill, ask if I wanted to look through them. I'd kneel on the floor and sort through the items, some of them with tags still on, feeling like I couldn't grab at too many. She'd pick out something that she thought would suit me, and I'd say yes, even when it was something I'd never wear. I'd taken home a white button-down shirt with a stiff collar, a blue cotton blazer as if I had some alternate professional life to wear it to. But in that moment, I couldn't have forced my lips to curl around the word *no*. When I looked around their apartment, my veins filled with rushes of want, as if I could see the price tags on everything, as if they would increase my own value, as if taking something else home would make it easier to pay rent. I picked up the skirt I'd taken home that first month: a knee-length striped skirt of metallic gold, snug around my thighs. I didn't know why I'd taken it, except for the fact that Nathalie had pointed to the label: "Missoni," she'd said. "Vintage!" That meant expensive, more so than any skirt I owned, and so I'd taken it, gingerly folded inside my purse, and reached in to pet it on the subway ride home.

I remembered coming home from weekends with my dad, the tension whenever I returned, clutching a gift.

Whatever he bought me ended up in a corner or a drawer. Now things from the Adriens cluttered my room in this way: lipsticks I'd never wear, bracelets with charms, a kitchen appliance grown dusty. I thought about gathering them in my arms and taking them to a consignment store. I looked again at the skirt, at its delicate gold threads creeping down the hip. The embroidery was so meticulous. When would I be given something like this again?

7
New York City, 2013

Nathalie often drank wine—in front of us and secretly, as I discovered in traces she left behind. I picked up glasses all over the house, sticky-sweet with residue and stained with red, as if a lipstick had melted around the bottom. Not wineglasses but espresso cups; clear, colored tumblers; stemless glasses like bowls. There was a row of sparkling crystal wineglasses displayed in the kitchen, but they looked too exquisite, like they were for special occasions.

She was making dinner for a couple who were coming over late. "They're flying in from London," Nathalie explained. "This was the only time they could do it, so at least if we cook, we'll be finished earlier, but then, you know, I have to cook." Bijou was in bed early, having already eaten a different meal from this one, which was lamb chops, potatoes smothered in rosemary, and a salad Nathalie would mix together with arugula and pine nuts. I felt like I was doing a good job helping her in the kitchen tonight. I'd successfully opened and closed the oven, used the meat thermometer, even chopped herbs for her.

Where was Gabe? I'd never been into the wing of the apartment that housed their bedroom; I didn't even know how big it was. I'd seen the hallway that led into it, which was where Nathalie's walk-in closet was. I couldn't remember if Nathalie had told me that their room was off-limits or if I'd assumed it was. She picked up her wine and took a sip and then looked at me. "Do you want a glass? I'm having some chardonnay." She turned and picked me out a stemless glass from the cupboard, the kind she was drinking from. "Here," she said. "Let me know if you like it." She sat on one of the barstools and motioned to the one next to her. "I have to wait for the lamb chops, then I'm all done," she said, reporting to herself.

I slid into the seat gingerly, taking the wine and sipping at it. I didn't actually like chardonnay, that strong buttery linger, but I wouldn't tell her. I liked the lightest and cheapest of sauvignon blancs, those cold red bubbly wines they sold in the summer, my neighborhood wine store's fifteen-dollar-and-under table. I knew that meant I didn't know enough to claim a preference.

"So." With a glass of wine in my hand, as if I were a friend, I felt emboldened to begin a conversation. "How do you know your friend who's coming?"

"Margot," she said. "We used to work together when we were babies—assistants. And her husband, Niall. They live here mostly, but Margot's from London, so they go back and forth." As she pronounced his name, she dragged out the first syllable with an unmistakable irritation—that, I recognized. The feeling of hating your friend's boyfriend. I didn't know how to ask her what was wrong with him, so I waited. "Ugh, he's okay, I guess," she said, backtracking. "He's gotten better, that's for sure."

"How did they meet?"

"Friends of friends, something like that, he's the type who's always around. He's a bit . . . traditional."

What was traditional code for? "In what way?" I asked carefully.

"He didn't want Margot to work after they got married, not that she minded, but he has these old-fashioned views. Politically . . . we try not to talk about it, but he's quite conservative. He held this lavish fundraiser in 2012. We thought it was in bad taste, to be so loud about it." She looked at me, as if measuring how this would fall into my ears. "Margot didn't agree, I don't think, but he's always been like that." She looked out the window and sighed. "But what can you do? She is an old friend, my first friend in New York, really. We try to get along. Oh—I should decant the wine," she said, still looking off.

"I can do it," I said quickly. I wanted a task to absorb me. "Open the wine?" They had a large and expensive wine opener that clamped around the bottle and opened it in two easy motions. I'd used it before to open cooking wine.

"Yes, and put it in the decanter. The wine's over there—with the red label. Oh—do you know how to open one?"

I nodded, of course, and looked for the clamp contraption.

"I'll dress the salad," she said, getting up from her barstool. "Here's the wine opener." She handed me a regular corkscrew. I took it from her with my eyes down; I had used a corkscrew but not that often. I inserted the screw into the cork carefully and twisted it in. Nathalie was standing a few feet away, turning over the salad in its large wooden bowl with her hands. When I went to pull the cork out, the dark red wine sprayed out and hit my chin. The counter gleamed with red drops.

"Oh, dear," she said. "You've pushed the cork down."

I felt the blood rush through my head. "I didn't—I did what I normally do."

"Well, I guess sometimes that happens," she said. Her hands were deep in the salad bowl, soaked in oil and parmesan, and she held them up to me as an excuse. "Can you grab—grab one of those chopsticks and push the cork further in. Then we can pour it out in the decanter, it'll be fine."

I took out a single chopstick from the drawer, black with tiny painted flowers. I poked at the cork tentatively, but it didn't budge. I saw Nathalie turn her head to wipe her cheek on her shoulder, and I pushed at the cork, heavily, with force. It popped into the bottle, and red wine spurted everywhere, splotches on the counter, in my hair, on my black sweater. It smelled dark and sweet, like dirt and sour candy. Nathalie turned, the gray sweater she had on streaked with red. I stopped, my mouth open. I felt the warm, confident bubble of five minutes ago pop loudly and certainly—permanently, maybe.

"Oh, it's fine, Willa. Pour it out into the decanter; we won't tell them how much is wasted." Her voice tinkled with sharp points, like icicles dripping cold. I did as she told me and asked if I could help with anything else. She turned to wash her hands at the sink.

"That's about it," she said. "Can you make sure Bijou doesn't need anything before you go? I have to get ready."

I waited for her to finish washing her hands and awkwardly placed the glass in the sink, not sure if I should wash it. Nathalie was looking out the window. "Thanks for the wine," I said quietly. I went to Bijou's room, where she was in her bed, playing a game on her iPad. I leaned in front of her.

"Do you need anything before I go home?"

She shook her head and raised a finger to my cheek. "Is that blood?" she said. I looked to the mirror next to her bed and saw a drop of red wine, crystallized on my cheek. I licked my own finger to wipe it off, and it left a pinkish smudge.

*

We were heading out of the school's revolving doors on a gloomy day when Bijou stopped short, her mouth in a tiny circle. "My science book," Bijou said. "I think I left it on the roof." There was no backyard for a playground, so Stanton had built it on top of the eight-story building. We headed up the eight flights of stairs, and as we neared the top, I heard high voices and laughter. I pushed open the door to a yellow jungle gym, a rack of orange swings, and a cluster of picnic tables.

"Where would your science book be?" I asked her.

"I thought I left it on the tables," she said, her voice small. I followed her gaze to the group of teenagers sitting on a picnic table. Stanton went until eighth grade, and I could tell from the stick legs and shiny foreheads that these must be the oldest kids, on the cusp of adolescence. Bijou moved behind me.

"Okay, I'll get it." I walked over to the kids. They straightened and sat up, as if they might be in trouble. "Have you guys seen a science textbook over here?"

They all looked at each other and then back at me and finally at the floor before shaking their heads in chorus.

"Nothing here," said the oldest-looking boy, the one with a crease in his forehead that he seemed to be trying to hold there.

Their noses were red, their hands jammed deep into pockets. With the clouds thick as blackout curtains, it felt chilly up here. "A little cold to be up here, isn't it?" I was surprised at how old and uncool I sounded, how they were treating me like a grown-up.

The same boy spoke. "Nowhere else to go," he said.

I turned away and walked Bijou back down the stairs. "Weird that they're sitting up there, right? Like they have nowhere else to hang out." She didn't answer. "Don't you feel like you have a lot of places to hang out?"

"Sure," she said.

"You're all lucky, you know, being in the city. There's so many places you can go. You know, where I grew up only had two streets of stores and restaurants and that was our *whole town*. We had to, like, hang out in the alley." Bijou put her thumbnail between her teeth, nibbling, and then stopped herself. "Maybe one of your teachers has it," I said finally.

"They don't," she said.

"Well, your mom will buy you a new one."

"She'll say I'm irresponsible," Bijou nearly shrieked. "She'll take something away."

"Can we stop into this coffee shop?" I asked her. My eyes were beginning to tingle with exhaustion, and my patience was draining.

She looked up at me sulkily. "If you say so."

"Do you want anything?" If she ordered something, then I could add mine to the reimbursement tally, but she shook her head. I got my coffee and went to the side to pour in milk. The girl standing there, adding sugar to her own coffee, was someone I'd seen before, around the neighborhood: at the corner store, walking to the subway. I thought she might be a server at the restaurant I could see from the Adriens' window. I smiled hesitantly, in recognition, and watched as she left.

"Do you know her?" Bijou said.

"No," I said quickly.

"She kind of looks like you," Bijou said.

I reached my hands to my cheeks, pressing on them with cool fingers. I felt stupid, but of course that was why I'd noticed her. She had dark hair, tan skin; she looked half something, half something else. And she was in this neighborhood because she was paid to be, not paying to be.

"You think so?" I said, putting the lid back on my coffee.

"Yeah, she's pretty," Bijou said. "What am I going to do? I wish you'd reminded me about my book before we left."

"How is this my fault?" I said.

"Whatever," she said, holding her backpack straps tightly as she trudged toward home.

*

Bijou was in the shower when Nathalie came home. I sat in the window nook, watching the last tendrils of sunset curl from the sky. Golden light dripped into cement. Bijou had been gloomy all night. I couldn't stop replaying this time when I was younger, climbing on the counters in my kitchen to get to the cereal when I knocked over a wide green bowl with my heel. It shattered on the kitchen floor seconds before my mom arrived home from work. My first instinct was to get rid of the evidence, and when I dropped to the floor, I'd sliced my palm open. I held it behind my back when my mom came in, bleeding into my shirt. I still had a faint white scar, a stripe under my thumb. When Nathalie asked me how my day was with Bijou, words left my mouth without my planning on them. I told her, "I accidentally left her science textbook in the coffee shop. I was carrying it for her."

*

When I got home, my apartment was empty, as usual. It felt as if Lucy had moved out. I turned on all the lights and dropped my purse in front of the door. If Lucy were coming home, I would have moved it, but she wasn't.

Lucy had lived here for years; the rent was low, the soft leather couch was left behind by her ex. I lived in what used to be his home office, big enough for a full-sized mattress and a secondhand dresser. And a bed frame, if I could ever find one. When I met Lucy at work, they'd broken up and she was looking for a new roommate. When I got to the apartment to look at it—a fourth-floor walk-up, fifteen minutes from the subway, no dishwasher, a sink that gave only scalding or ice-cold—I knew I'd say yes, for the company, for the way Lucy had clutched my wrist when I told her I would come check it out. I hadn't expected her eagerness to transfer so quickly to someone else.

I opened the fridge; I'd eaten with Bijou earlier, but I felt hungry again. There was a container of fried rice, and I picked at it without heating it up, the voices from the television echoing off the walls. I had people I could meet for a drink, but I would have had to text them days in advance, make plans, fit myself into their calendar and them into mine. I didn't have friends I could just *see.* I'd glanced into the bars I'd passed on my walk home from the subway, looking at the groups of people huddled over wineglasses and candles, feet dangling off barstools, wrists and elbows colliding, speaking without thinking, laughing without swallowing, like it was nothing, like it was easy to find somewhere to belong.

8

Kent, New York, 2005

On the seventh day of a two-month summer at my dad's, I finally found the sunscreen. In the morning, I massaged cold white cream everywhere, from hips to ankles, circling shoulders, pressing it into the spaces between my toes. I stood in front of the mirror and stared at the gradient changes in my skin—the pale white shapes of necklines and bikini bottoms, the clean loop left behind from a hair tie on my wrist, so white and bright they looked reflective, impossible. I had never been as white as those outlines made it seem.

My mom said it would be good for me to spend two full months with him, which I'd never done before. It was a break from being around her newborn, but still, I had nothing to do but sit in his backyard and read, baking my skin in the July sun. I hadn't known where the sunscreen was, and as the week went on, it felt too late to ask.

I hadn't spoken to anyone outside of my dad's house since the day he picked me up, when I'd walked into my mom's town in the morning to buy an iced coffee. Normally I didn't like to be seen alone, but that day I felt okay about it, because I was about to leave. I'd never left Durland for this long, and in two months, I might come back a different person—still sixteen, but in a different way. But one week in, and I had been mostly sitting by myself, reading and picking at my skin. In some ways, it was a relief to be ignored. Back home, whenever I went to the mall or the movie theater or to CVS, people stared and asked me where I was from. Even when I answered, *Here, I was born here, I've lived in this town my whole life*, they pressed on, guessing. *Are you Filipina? Mexican? Hawaiian?* Strangers wanted to know if I was born abroad or if I spoke another language. To tell me that I reminded them of their manicurist or their housekeeper or their brother's new wife. Sometimes they'd swear they knew someone who looked just like me, and that was why they *had* to come up and speak to me. If I hadn't learned how anything past a polite laugh would sear them to my side, then I might have asked to see these people they knew who looked like me; might have asked for proof that I wasn't alone.

*

My dad was frying eggs for everyone, so when I walked into the kitchen, he fried me some too. After pushing plates toward his daughters, he plucked two from the carton—a muddy-colored cardboard package, not that Easter-pink foam we bought at my mom's. The eggs hissed when they hit the skillet, four breakfasts in, and two slices of bread popped up out of the toaster. I wondered if they'd been for him or if he'd remembered me.

There were three stools at the counter, and his daughters were at two of them. My stepmother was at the kitchen table, one leg folded into the crook of her arm as she flipped through a glossy magazine. Her picked-over plate was pushed to the side—toast with two round bites in it, an egg cut into many pieces.

He pushed a plate toward the last empty stool, and I edged onto the seat to pull it toward me. The eggs were fried, lacy brown edges curling up. I could tell that when I tapped at them with my fork, a chalky yellow would flake off rather than spill out. It was how the girls were eating theirs. I didn't know how to tell him I only liked soft, runny yolks—the kind that flooded onto everything around them. I remembered poached, over easy, even scrambled, from the times he'd picked me up and taken me to diners for breakfast. I remembered soft white toast, not whole wheat, and black coffee, though what I saw at the house was half-and-half and hazelnut creamer. I'd spent all of our weekends and holidays memorizing what he liked, and here, in his house, I saw I didn't truly know. I sectioned off a piece of egg white with a crispy brown edge. I nibbled at the butter-glistening toast balanced on the side. Then I sank my fork into the pale crayon yolk.

"Daddy, too much butter," Charlotte said. "Can you make me different toast?" I watched her carefully, how those words didn't bother her at all.

"I love butter," Esther said. She grabbed Charlotte's, turned the toast upside down, and placed the soft, soaked-through side straight onto her tongue.

"More toast," he said, pulling out two soft pieces of bread from the bag on the counter.

With my elbows on the counter, I watched everyone in their places. They were a beautiful family, a diverse denim ad, my dad broad-shouldered and brown-skinned, with his hummingbird women perched all around. Though

Charlotte and Esther should have looked like me, mixed, they appeared to me more naturally so, like someone had stirred their palettes for long enough, like they had waited for their portraits to set.

"What are you going to do today?" Cynthia asked me, like she did every day, as if it were a real question, when she knew there was nothing I could say. I didn't have my license yet. I didn't know anyone here. The center of town was almost nine miles away, too far to walk. She wanted me to say that I had nothing to do, as if it made me lazy instead of trapped. Charlotte and Esther were in summer school, not for being bad at classes but for being good, in some kind of advanced academic track that signaled their promise.

I looked at my dad, but he was turned toward the stove, with his back to me. I took another bite so I could pull my shoulders up and down instead of talking, and the yolk moistened slowly on top of my tongue. Cynthia took in this gesture and looked back at her magazine. She'd suggested that I, too, go to summer school while I was here, but it was an empty proposal she didn't want to enforce. It wasn't like I could sit next to my younger sisters at another activity they tried to include me in, six years past normalcy, reciting math I'd learned and forgotten years before. They'd tried this with swimming, gymnastics, a single tennis lesson. I still didn't know how to swim.

I'd been trying to count how many words I spoke at each meal, telling myself that I should participate more, but it was hard when they were standing around the kitchen island, responding to starts of sentences I didn't know the ends to. I observed their daily rituals. They pinched the backs of each other's elbows. They knew who wanted pepper closest to their place setting. They mixed salad with their hands and placed the leaves straight onto each other's tongues. And they didn't look anything like me, Charlotte and Esther with Cynthia's angular cheekbones, her long neck. My dad was tan and so was I, though his older sisters were both paler. Charlotte and Esther looked more like that, but whether it was our shared aunts, their half-white genetics, or their sun-shaded practice, I didn't know. Before they left the house, Cynthia slid sunscreen onto their foreheads and noses, like she was touching them with a cross.

Charlotte and Esther scraped back their seats to go get ready for their day. My dad took a plate for himself to the table where Cynthia was, but the movement looked unpracticed, like he was imposing. Maybe he usually sat at the counter where I was. Cynthia scooted her chair over a little, to make room. I choked down most of my meal and felt like I should get up too, but I stayed for a moment, my ankles hooked around each other. My dad cut into his own eggs, and I watched as they poured out sunny yellow yolk, oozing all the way to the plate's gold-patterned edge.

*

I was sent here ostensibly to spend time with my dad, but I mostly spent the days alone, avoiding his wife. During the week he'd leave right after breakfast, which I'd sometimes tug myself from bed for, and he'd come back when I was already so lethargic that I couldn't muster any enthusiasm to strengthen our relationship or whatever. They lived an hour away from where I lived with my mom, in a house with three stories, two extra bedrooms, and sun-drenched yards in back and front. The driveways in their neighborhood were a quarter mile of gravel before you reached the front door. I couldn't imagine anyone walking up and down, trick-or-treating or selling knives. I didn't know how to get anywhere but their mailbox on the street.

The bedroom I stayed in here had white sheets, a white comforter, and whispery curtains that filtered in summer sun. Nighttime didn't come until nine, and then the moon hung in front of my window, a stubborn night-light I couldn't unplug. It was a strange house. Everyone ran around asking each other questions that stemmed from some earlier conversation they remembered. *Was it veal or chicken? Which part of the vocabulary worksheet? What did Mrs. Malone say about my cauliflower? What time do you want to go to Red's? Did you tell Lauren's mom what I said about field day? Where's that Tupperware I gave you last Wednesday? Have you called Jeff about the pool?*

Everyone asked each other questions, but no one asked much of me.

*

When Esther invited me into her room, I lowered myself lightly onto the side of her bed, a four-poster pink frame with curtains hanging around it, like a princess's in a coloring book. Esther opened her closet as soon as I came inside. She wanted to show me her clothes. I stood up and touched the cherry-red blazers hanging in a row.

"Those are my uniforms," she said. "Charlotte has a different one, a vest instead of a jacket, and her skirt gets to be shorter. I have to wait two years." I pulled one of the hangers out to look at the crest on the side. "Do you have a school uniform?"

"Public schools don't have uniforms, really."

"The luckiest," she said, turning with a huff and sorting through her things.

"It's not that great," I said, putting her jacket back.

"What's it like?" She turned away from the closet and sat on a bench at the foot of her bed. "Public school."

"Well, the food sucks," I said. "No one ever eats the food we get at school. We walk into town and buy pizza or something. The only food at school that's edible is the chocolate chip cookies."

"We're not even allowed to leave school." Her eyes were wide. "At *all*."

"But I bet you have good lunch food." Actually, only seniors could leave at lunchtime, so I had only snuck off a few times. I wasn't sure why the lie floated from my mouth, as if to impress her. I turned back to her closet and clicked through the hangers.

"Having cookies for lunch sounds better."

"You guys have way more vacation time. I got out of school two weeks ago."

Disbelief covered her face. "We've been out since May."

I nodded solemnly. "Exactly. What's that?" Deep in the back of her closet, a tuft of fabric gleamed between the uniforms and pastel dresses, a shiny deep crimson color like a ruby dirtied with oil.

Esther stood up to maneuver the dress out. "It's my Christmas dress. From last year. Nai Nai made them for us. Maybe Mom still has yours. Nai Nai made you one, too, because she forgot you wouldn't be here. It was an odd year."

I'd never thought of it like that: since I switched off holidays at my parents' houses, I supposed the years *were* always even when I was here. Esther said it like we all knew.

"So you'll be here this year for Christmas, right? I asked Nai Nai this year to not make us ones with lace collars. It's *so* Victorian." She pinched the collar of last year's dress, and I reached out to do the same.

"I think it's kind of pretty," I said. "Like a doll."

There was a flash and a quick whir behind us, and I turned. Charlotte was standing in the doorway with a slim silver camera. "Got you," she said.

"*Charlotte,*" Esther wailed, her voice high and hysterical. "I told you not to do it when I wasn't ready!"

"But it's no good if you're ready. I like a natural subject," Charlotte said. She looked down at the screen with satisfaction. "Here, I'll show you. Smile?"

Esther looked distressed, but obediently stretched her mouth. She was one of those children who hadn't really learned how to smile, more of a rectangle than a citrus wedge. I also turned to Charlotte and smiled woodenly. *Click, whir.* Charlotte walked to us and held the screen in front of us. "See the difference?" she said. In the smiling picture, Esther and I looked like two people who didn't know each other, caught somewhere like a dental office. Then Charlotte clicked to the picture before. The dress was positioned perfectly in the center of the frame, and you could see both of our profiles, both of our hands as we reached out to touch it. We looked like we were in the middle of something, busy dressmakers discussing a fabric we might use. We looked in process. I felt someone taking a picture of me was a kindness, especially one in which I didn't look uncomfortable. "Want me to take one of you two?" I said.

"Nah," Charlotte said, scrolling through her photos. "Right now I'm taking only photos where people can't see where I'm coming from. Like I'm a spy. Here, look." She held the screen in front of me, and I saw here what I'd been wanting to know: what the family looked like, what they did when they weren't doing it in front of me. Here was my dad cleaning the pool in swim trunks and a T-shirt. Here was my dad reading a thick paperback in bed past a half-open door. Here was Cynthia in her bathroom, tapping moisturizer under her eyes. Here was Esther stirring cereal. Here was Esther putting her hand up at the lens. Here was Esther, mid-scream.

"Is this your camera?" I asked.

"It was my mom's, but she never used it. Now it's mine. I'm going to be a photographer," she said proudly. She continued to scroll through the photos, showing me. It wasn't that they were all good; there were shots of someone's elbow, of her socks in bed, an ice cream carton with a spoon sticking out. But there was also my dad, getting out of his car. I wondered how Charlotte had even gotten such a high angle, her camera lens above him. He was looking up, smiling, in an everyday kind of way, like he wasn't annoyed by it but a little bemused, a rolling-his-eyes kind of smile. The kind you'd give to someone you saw six hours out of every day. I squeezed my eyes shut for a moment. When I opened them, Charlotte had clicked on. Here was Esther, watching TV on her stomach. Here was Cynthia, brushing Esther's hair.

9

New York City, 2013

"Le Pain Quotidien? Au Bon Pain? Pret a Manger? *Nothing* with a French name? How about Chipotle?" I was trying to get Bijou to pick somewhere to eat lunch. "Burger King?" Her eyebrows inched up. "Have you ever even tried Burger King?"

Bijou had a half day because there was a teachers' conference. *Take her out to eat somewhere and to a museum or something*, Nathalie had texted me. *You still have my credit card, right?* I loved when Nathalie didn't give me too many directions, when I had free rein to play house. I'd been early to pick Bijou up and had scrolled through the news on my phone. Each day, more and more horrible things happened: children went missing, homes were robbed, people were killed by construction accidents or errant cars or the police. By the time Bijou had come out, I was feeling twitchy, protective. I'd looked at the braid tucked inside her jacket and thought that being a mother must be devastating. I'd pulled it out of her collar gently and asked where she wanted to go.

"I don't want to decide on lunch until I know what we're doing *after* lunch," she said, and I went back to feeling annoyed by her. These tragedies never occurred in her padded, pastel world. We were leaning against the brick wall of the school as her friends walked out with their nannies or mothers, waving at us. On the corner, a cop knelt down to retrieve a highlighter a student had dropped. It was Wednesday, the free day of Bijou's schedule.

"I know!" she said."I really want to go to the botanical garden. The one in the Bronx."

"We are not going to the Bronx," I said. "That would be like two hours on the train."

"The one in Brooklyn, then!" she said, pleading. "My art teacher told me about it. I've never been there."

"That's far, too, Bee," I said. "I don't know if we have time."

"Let's look it up on your phone," she suggested. "I don't think it's that far from here. Isn't it off the 2/3?"

Without looking, I knew she was right. It would take thirty minutes on the train. "It's a little cold to be at the garden," I said. "Your mom said we should go to a museum. How about we go to the New Museum? They have this giant rose sculpture in front this month. It'll be even better than the garden. And warmer. Plus—that's right by that café you love! Lila's."

"*You* love Lila's," she said.

"You like it too, don't lie. Didn't you like that spicy hot chocolate with the big marshmallow?"

"Okay, fine," she said. "Only if I can have one of those."

I breathed out, relieved. "Of course you can," I said.

"Mom would probably, like, kill you, if you took me to Burger King," she said idly as we crossed the street.

"Oh, would she?"

"Did your mom let you eat Burger King?"

"Yeah, but everyone's mom did," I said. "It's not going to literally kill you."

"I think it's more that it slowly kills you," she said. "Fast food."

"Have you always been a picky eater?"

"I'm not picky! I eat everything."

"Everything expensive."

She kicked at a rock with her sneaker. "I like breakfast cereal," she said.

Lila's was a tiny slice of a café on a side street in Soho, with rickety black tables set up on a tiled floor. They were uncomfortable to sit at but relayed a kind of Parisian chic vibe. Each time we went, we both got the salmon sandwich. It came on thick, seeded bread with mayonnaise they called aioli and tomato slices that spurted seeds. The salmon was poached, the way Bijou liked it, the way I protested making it because you had to peel off the glittering charcoal skin.

"Do you really think I'm picky?" Bijou said as she drank her hot chocolate.

"No, I was just kidding," I said. "It's more that you have a sophisticated palate."

"You know I'm going to have a restaurant one day, right?"

"I didn't know. But I'm sure you will." I was—sure that it would happen. After we finished our sandwiches, the empty afternoon stretched in front of us. I gave Bijou the chocolate that came with the bill. The sun was streaming through the windows, shadows from the hanging plants trembling across the floor. I was getting paid extra today. "Maybe we can go to the garden next week," I said generously. "Should we head to the museum?"

*

I knew going to museums was a luxury, of time and proximity, but I was getting bored with them. The paintings all seemed to blur together. I wished someone would tell me what to see. Bijou liked to take the elevator to the top floor and then walk our way down. This one was small, so I knew we couldn't be here that long. As I trailed behind Bijou's braid and jacket, her backpack slung over my shoulder, my temples began to pulse, and a space in my stomach started to announce itself, whirring, swaying. I wondered if I was really feeling this or if I was making myself feel it by being bored, by thinking about how I felt. I distrusted myself in this essential way; I couldn't believe what I felt unless someone else confirmed it. *I'm probably fine*, I thought. I sat on a nearby couch and thought I would rest for a minute, until I could move my mind past it. A few minutes later, Bijou ran up to me.

"I think I'm going to be sick," she said.

I looked into her eyes and saw myself reflected back in her pupils. "I think me too."

I was glad we'd gone to the museum as we rushed into the large, clean bathroom. I knelt on the floor, feeling the cold marble through my jeans, and lunch fell from my mouth. Next to me were Bijou's school shoes; she wasn't kneeling. Nathalie was going to kill me. My stomach emptied and churned, and hot tears fell from the corners of my eyes.

I thought of what would happen at the apartment. Nathalie surprised me sometimes with her reactions to things. You could see from any little detail of her that she was clean and composed: her hair, sleek and glossy at any time of the day; her giant engagement ring, hanging ever so slightly to the left; the way her clothes fit her perfectly, as if she got every T-shirt and cardigan tailored to her frame; and the way they were never wrinkled, even when she'd been sitting cross-legged for hours. But then sometimes she would lean over and scoop gunk out of Bijou's eyes with her pinky finger, she'd take a tissue and dig up into Bijou's nostrils, she'd mix ground beef with her hands wrist-deep in a silver bowl—she was a mother, and mothers got their hands dirty with their kids. I knew that. Certain things didn't faze her, but it was like I never knew what would be too much. She hadn't been happy with me lately. I had been late to pick Bijou up after getting stuck on the subway last week. I had burned the turkey meatloaf a few days ago. I had broken a water glass yesterday—it had fallen from my grip as if my fingers had been oiled and smashed into a dozen pieces on the kitchen floor. And now—this.

*

I thought impossibly about leaving before Nathalie got home, and not having to face her. Maybe Gabe would come home early from his work trip and dismiss me. After we took a cab home and I put Bijou in bed, I sat on the couch nervously, waiting. When the elevator sounded, I stood up. Nathalie smiled distantly as she walked in, undoing her jacket, nudging off her heels. Maybe I could say nothing, I thought hopefully, pretend that Bijou was just tired, and leave before she noticed. But before I could lose my nerve, I said to her, "I think we, um, I think we may have food poisoning."

"*Food poisoning?* What did you give her for lunch?"

My stomach began to churn again in the pit below my rib cage, and I had to turn from her into the nearest bathroom. I gagged into the toilet before I could turn the sink on to mask the noise. After I flushed, I looked at my arms and then in the mirror; I'd broken out into a cold sweat that coated my body with a thick film. I wiped my arms with the dainty white hand towel hanging near the sink and, for a moment, considered throwing it away. I heard Nathalie call for Bijou and open her door. I took a moment to splash water on my face and dry it. My face looked zombielike, hollow.

"What did Willa give you for lunch?" Nathalie was asking Bijou, bringing the edge of the comforter to her chin.

"Um, Nathalie," I said from the door of Bijou's room. "I can go if you want. I think you only wanted me until five today?"

"Okay. Let me give you cab fare, I don't know that you should ride the subway. Well—" Nathalie looked up at me. "Is your roommate home?"

"Probably not," I said.

Bijou kicked the covers off, mumbling that she was too hot. Nathalie bent over Bijou's legs and peeled off her socks, one by one, and balled them up, held the damp hot things tight in her fist. Then she looked back at me, my body covered again with sweat, and my whole body vibrated with want, with a yearning that I didn't know the name of.

"You should stay, Willa," she said. "You don't look so well, and I wouldn't want you to get worse all alone. You can stay in the guest room."

My throat opened, then closed, like a flower that bloomed early, then remembered the frost.

"Stay, Willa," Bijou said. "It's safer." I was used to hearing Bijou talking about safety when it pertained to knives, subway poles, or undercooked meat, but not me.

The guest room had a bed and a sofa. Bijou walked me there, and then she lay on the sofa. "I'll lie here for a little," she said. I sat on the bed. Nathalie came in and gave me a change of clothes—her clothes. "These might be more comfortable for you," she said. I held them in my hands—a pair of pajama pants, white-and-blue striped, a soft jersey cotton, a little white drawstring; a plain white T-shirt; a gray zip-up sweatshirt. "There's a bathroom right there you can change in. Bijou, let's get up and give Willa space."

"Oh, it's okay," I said quickly. "She can stay if she wants." I tightened my grip on the pajamas, as if she might take them back.

"I'll be right outside. I'll be back to check on you," Nathalie said. *You*, meaning both of us.

*

When I emerged from the bathroom once again, Nathalie was sitting on the bed, watching Bijou sleep on the sofa. She'd put a cloth over her forehead. "I don't want to move her," she said. "She should sleep as much as she can. How are you? That sounded painful. Come lie down. I'll do you too." She had brought in a bowl of water, and she dipped a washcloth into it, then folded it over my forehead. The cold felt holy, unbelievable in its relief. "It's hard to be alone when you're sick," she said. "I'm glad that you stayed." Her voice was light, honeyed, as I'd never heard her before. Who was this?

When I looked up at her, I thought of my mother. I remembered being young, before Ray, and my mother letting me spend the whole day in her bed when I was sick, turning on the TV and bringing me soup and running her hands all over my body, testing the glands on my neck and gently pressing at my temples and feeling my forehead. "Won't you get sick?" I asked her. "How won't you get sick?"

"I'm your mother," she'd say, like it was a cross she held in front of her body, a garland of garlic strung around her neck.

Nathalie left me with the compress on my forehead. At some point, Bijou climbed into the bed. It was a queen-size bed, and her body was far away from mine. We fell asleep that way. The night darkened. The sheets were so soft inside the tall, glossy bed frame. I spread my arms out as I usually did, and when my left arm fell off the side, it dangled luxuriously in the air. I was used to knocking my knuckles on the floor. *I wonder where this bed frame is from*, I thought, and then I fell into a sticky molasses sleep. I heard Nathalie open and then close the door, but rather than be awakened by the interruption, I was plunged even further into sleep each time she checked on us.

*

Maybe I wasn't a good nanny. I barely thought about Bijou. I remembered her taking on a waterlogged quality, her skin with the slightest blue tint, her round marble eyes cracking with red, but was this how she'd looked in reality or how she'd looked in my sleep-state, the two of us held underwater by the same wave? After I felt better, I realized that I had not felt concerned about Bijou, not in the way I should have, as her paid caregiver. I had been thinking of myself, how all of it was my fault because I chose the lunch place, and I was going to head home on the subway by myself, walking in a swishing unsteady line, how I wanted to have a mother to return to. But Nathalie asked me to stay. And then I had thought only of her.

10

Durland, New Jersey, 1998

My mom had a garden, and it was wild and green. The other houses in our town had clean manicured plots of flowers with straight stems pointing to the sky, lots of tulips and miniature pink flower buds that she told me were called touch-me-nots. None of the flowers in my mom's garden had names that were easy to remember. There were no polite infusions of blush and ribbon yellow, but instead six shades of green holding up shoots of deep purple, sunset pink, indigo blue, all bending and sprawling, leaning so far into the driveway the buds would scrape her car as we pulled in, turning our small yard junglelike, so that when we sat at our outdoor table, we had to push the flowers from our faces. She had a buddleia butterfly bush that dripped out purple flowered cones; thick white peonies with petals layered like wedding cakes; a climbing hydrangea vine that took over the entire backside of our house with its green leaves and white blossoms; hot-pink azaleas, loud like lipstick in the summer; lady's mantle, a lime-green bush that bloomed in tiny, hairy clumps; and my favorite, the blue balloon flower. It grew with its petals fused together like the outline of a hot-air balloon, and when it was ready, its petals popped open to reveal a starburst shape.

My mom wanted the garden to be special, distinct from the neighborhood, and she spent time on it. She was always elbow-deep in the soil, her knees caked in dirt, and coming into the house with fingernails rimmed in black. I didn't like getting dirty the same way, but sometimes she would coax me to join her, and I'd plunge my arms into the cold, spongy earth beside her.

As summer edged closer, the balloon flowers would ripen into their puffed-up balls, and though we could wait for them to open, we could also go out and pop them open ourselves. My mom would take me outside, and I'd gently squeeze one between my thumb and pointer finger. If you weren't gentle, the petals would rip, so I held them between my finger pads, as if I were holding a single drop of water. With a nudge, the petals popped open to a five-pointed star, deep blue with purple veins. As if it had been waiting for my touch.

We often went to nearby nurseries, where she'd drag a wagon behind her, picking up terra-cotta planters and placing them in. Every couple of months, we'd drive to Brooklyn or the Bronx. She spent hours at the botanical gardens, reading the signs carefully, touching petals with reverence. It was where she got ideas for her garden, she said. I fell asleep on benches in the sun, waiting. After my dad left, the inside of the house never changed. She had the same bed, the same couch, the same TV, the same kitchen table, even after Ray moved in. But the backyard became more and more flowered each year. That part was hers. Her garden, wild and green—vibrant and unruly, tangled, but alive.

11

New York City, 2013

I woke up in the guest room, and Bijou was gone. The curtains were fully drawn, sun sloshing across the bed. I lay there on my back, smoothed my arms down on the comforter, and looked around. There were three framed pictures on the wall, a tufted satin bench at the foot of the bed, a tall ivory dresser with drawers closed and no clutter on the top. I had this superstition that if I wanted something too explicitly, if I let my mind focus on the words, I would jinx myself. I often let my desires stay murky and unvoiced. But that morning, I pinched the smooth duvet cover between my fingers and let it drop, and I thought, *I wish that I lived here too.*

I felt briefly suspended inside those words, but then I lifted myself to my elbows and swung my legs over the side to stand up. Raw stomach, dry mouth, two sharp pulsing points for temples, but I was well enough to go home. I changed back into the clothes I'd worn yesterday and worried about what to say when I walked into the living room. It was a familiar feeling; I'd mostly lived in apartments in which I felt uncomfortable in the common space, having to prep myself with talking points before I walked in. I had roommates who lounged in their underwear, cooking lazily, taking up space, but I scurried from bedroom to kitchen to bathroom and back. Now, since Lucy was never home, I did finally have that sense of space and laziness I'd coveted, but it was lonelier than I thought.

When I checked my phone, I saw a text from Nathalie. Gabe was out of town this week so she'd taken Bijou to the doctor. *Just in case*, she wrote. I walked out into the empty apartment. There were a throw blanket and two pillows scattered on the floor in front of the couch, a mug half-full on the coffee table. I had been here by myself before. It felt different today.

*

I didn't come back until the following Monday, when the sickness felt like a distant memory, something I was embarrassed about, how sweaty and weak I had been. I waited for Bijou outside her classroom, unsure how to bring it up.

"How are you feeling?" I said finally as we walked to dance. "All better? Are you sure you're up for dance class?" Nathalie had told me I could stay home so I could rest, and that she'd stay home with Bijou, but it felt to me like I was being banished, as if what I had was contagious. Four straight days in Brooklyn and I'd wished that Bijou had her own phone, that I could text her to ask how she was, to see if she felt the same way as I did.

"I was almost all better by the following day, Mom was just being extra careful," she said primly, as if we were all overreacting. "But I can't believe that we both got food poisoning from that sandwich. We should sue them."

"Lila's?"

"Their sandwich made us sick."

"I don't think that would do anything," I said. Could you sue a restaurant for something like that? "We've had that sandwich like ten times. Sometimes things just happen."

"I don't think I'll *ever* eat salmon again," she said.

I'd had a salmon-avocado roll the night before. "We'll see. You might forget."

We walked on silently a few more blocks until we reached the dance studio. I pulled the door open for her. She paused while walking in and looked up at me. "I think they should know that they hurt us," she said.

*

At the end of the week, Nathalie called me into the kitchen, where she was standing on one side of the counter, drinking wine.

"Willa," she said. "Gabe and I have been talking."

I stood on the other side of the counter from her, waiting quietly amid the hum of the appliances, the refrigerator breathing, the dishwasher whirring in waves. What had I done?

"Remember how I told you we might want a live-in nanny down the road?" She enunciated *live-in nanny* crisply, as if she remembered me asking what it meant. "We've decided that's what we need this year for Bijou. Gabe has been traveling more, I always travel, his mother is having a little health thing, and we need someone constant for her."

I felt needled, but nodded. I was being dismissed? I looked to my hands, then to Nathalie's, on the other side of the counter. I saw again her star tattoo and thought darkly how stupid it was. Why did she get to act like every decision of hers was final, perfect?

"I could be the live-in nanny." I was worried she could hear how desperate I felt.

"Well, I wasn't sure if you were interested in that. I have some other names—girls with experience. It's more than you're doing now. It would mean getting her up in the morning, taking her to school, certain weekends . . . it's more than just afternoons. It's not for everyone."

I knew that was true. It was for the women I saw at Bijou's school, waiting outside with granola bars in the pockets of their Columbia sweatshirts, extra water bottles and hand sanitizer and folding umbrellas in their totes.

"But I could do it," I said.

She cleared her throat, then looked at me. "You've never lived with a family before, have you?"

"No," I said. Wholly, honestly. "But I've always wanted to."

Nathalie was someone who never rushed to fill a silence. She pushed herself slightly away from the counter, watching me, seeing what I might do.

"Bijou likes me," I said.

"Bijou likes you," she repeated. It was so hard to read her tone when her voice never wavered. Was she agreeing with me or taunting me? "Well, in the end that's all that matters, isn't it?"

*

I got on the subway home feeling like I'd won. But as the train swerved, I wondered what it was I'd attained. Nathalie had insisted I take a week to think about it, and went over the particulars: what time I'd have to wake up to take Bijou to school; how weekends would be free unless scheduled in advance; that time off could be discussed; how they'd mostly cover groceries, but I could have a shelf in the kitchen for my own food outside of the kitchenette. I felt embarrassed, the way I always did after I made a choice. Had it been the right one?

*

When Lucy finally came home, it was day five of my week of thinking about it. I woke up to her grinding coffee beans, and when I walked out, she told me she was leaving soon. "What are you doing today? Work?" she asked.

"Yeah, I'll leave around two," I said. She nodded, opening the cabinets and pulling out boxes. Looking for something, but I didn't know what. "Actually, she, uh—the mom actually asked me something the other night. I guess they want a live-in nanny now."

"Do they want you to do that?" There was an emphasis on the *you.*

I nodded. "Maybe—well, she said I could think about it and stay on for another month no matter what, so I'd have lots of time to find something else. They have this big, like, guest-room wing in their apartment. It has its own bathroom and mini-kitchen, and rent is included."

"Do they change your hourly rate?" Lucy asked.

I wasn't sure. "I think it's the same."

"But you'll get more hours, right? Plus, you don't have to pay rent?"

I realized I was telling Lucy because I had expected her to scoff at it—to talk me out of it. I'd felt so warmed by the idea of a new life, the sun shining hot and yellow on all the luxuries I'd inherit by living there. But as Lucy banged cabinets closed, I felt like the sun had fallen behind a cloud, and I could think only of the gloom. No privacy, no escape. She reached into the fridge and pulled out a small carton of creamer. Who would I talk to?

"I feel like I'd live almost anywhere for zero rent," she said, stirring her cup with one finger. "But in Manhattan, even? I mean, kind of too good to pass up, huh?"

"You said you don't even like Manhattan, though." My voice was small. It was the kind of thing people said, I knew, when they couldn't afford to be there.

"Well, you know. Obviously we aren't on a lease. Aaron and I have been talking about—not super seriously but—you know, about me moving into his place. I mean, when would they want you to move in by?"

I wished I hadn't said anything, that I'd sat alone to weigh the options, but what could I do but answer her? "A month," I said. "So—well, end of November, beginning of December."

"Oh, that would be perfect," she said. "I'm sick of the water pressure here, aren't you? I'm going to talk to Aaron before I call Jim, but maybe we can both move out then and be done with it." Jim, our landlord.

She put the creamer back on the shelf and closed the fridge, and a Polaroid fell off from behind three others. We didn't have enough magnets to keep everything in place. I leaned down to pick it up. I'd forgotten about this one.

Lucy's red hair was smoothed into twenties waves, and she was wearing red lipstick and a black off-the-shoulder dress, her collarbone arched forward while she pouted. I was next to her in a crewneck sweatshirt with no makeup on, laughing and looking her way, as she held the camera in front of us with two arms. When I'd moved in, Lucy had a goal of submitting to three auditions a week. She had been in one commercial for prescription eye drops and a handful of ads, and said that she couldn't lose her momentum. In order to get submitted for an audition, she usually had to tape herself reading some of the lines, wearing the type of outfit they might like. On our days off, or after we got home from work, she always pulled me into it.

"Do you think you could help me with something?" she'd say shyly. "I made breakfast to thank you!" And she'd unveil something like chocolate chip pancakes, or french toast, something I never told her I didn't like. If it was after work, she'd blend frozen margaritas or make us cocktails. I didn't mind helping her with the tapes. What else did I have to do? Sometimes if someone asked me what I'd done the day before, I'd talk about the tape we made for Lucy. *It's for this cool indie film where she'd be playing this . . .*

"I'm supposed to be in high school," she'd say, and we'd push a headband on her head and button up a sweater to the top. "I'm supposed to be like, the evil best friend, who seduces her friend's boyfriend?" And we'd find something low-cut, or tight—stereotypical, obvious; she said this was what they wanted. Then I'd read the other part's lines as I held her digital camera to film her side. I spent months like this, helping her with her auditions, and she'd say, "You really are the best," to me. "I'll do this for you, whenever you want." And I believed it. That all I had to do was figure out what I wanted, and I'd have Lucy there, ready to do half the work. I often found myself in friendships with people like this, self-absorbed and sparkling. It took the pressure off me when everyone was looking at them. But it curdled into resentment, for how neatly I clicked into the slot of sidekick, for how quickly they cast me there.

I put the picture back on the fridge. Lucy flashed a bright smile at me and continued getting ready to leave.

*

On the last day before I moved out, I stopped into a coffee shop that I didn't normally go to. From the window outside, it looked so crowded, but when I stepped in I realized there was a back section through a hallway with plenty of seating. The room was covered in plants, hanging from ceiling beams and stacked on the floor. There was one long communal table where several people sat reading or typing into computers. Soft indie rock played on the speakers. I walked toward an empty corner of the long table. A woman with long hair and jade hoops noticed me walking and moved her books and her muffin over a few inches before I even sat down. She didn't say anything, just kindly made space for me. I sat down and smiled at her. She returned it and went back to her book. I felt an uneasy warmth, a tinge of regret, the rush of caffeine, the dance of my nerves. *New life starts tomorrow.*

*

The move was not hard. The room was already furnished and contained nicer things than my old room had. I'd put my dresser and a couple of things on Craigslist and collected cash for them. The Adriens were going upstate until Sunday to visit Gabe's parents for Thanksgiving. This seemed like the only chance to move in alone, without them watching me pad my way in nervously, without them watching me walk out to the kitchen for a snack. I thought it would help me feel comfortable to move in while they were away.

I arrived at their building with a suitcase, two bags, and an open box with some books and a framed photo. My favorite doorman, James, helped get my things from the trunk of the cab and bring them up. He was young, around my age, and he was studying for his real estate license, though he said even when he passed he'd still work here until his sales started to take off. I envied the viability of his plan, the clear path. I wondered if he envied me my temporary crowning as resident, or if he could see the strings.

The elevator doors opened, and he left my things in the foyer with me. When they closed, I tried out a new truth: "I'm home," I said, but it came out in a whisper. Usually on Thanksgiving and Christmas, I would go to my mom's or my dad's. I'd told them via text that I'd gotten a new job, that I had to move over the weekend, and I'd be working on Thanksgiving. That night, after I'd unpacked some of my things and looked in the fridge, where there were leftovers and cold cuts and juice and fruit, I piled my plate and sat at the kitchen counter, staring at the darkened skyline of buildings. I squinted at the windows with lights on, imagining what was going on behind them. I looked down at the plate, my appetite murky where it had been pronounced. I took a picture of the view and texted each of my parents. Watching my phone for a response, I ate mechanically, trying to coax myself into the hunger I had so recently felt. *What am I doing here?* I thought, shifting in my seat as I looked around at the large, empty room.

12

Durland, New Jersey, 2004

My childhood bedroom had white wallpaper with tiny blue and green flowers on it. My mom had picked it out. Everyone else I knew had a painted room, pale pink or light blue or pastel green. I picked at the vertical seams with my fingers, tried to peel it down. I had a white bed with a round headboard, something I'd circled in a catalog in sixth grade and asked my mom to buy me for months, with a matching desk. She'd told me she wouldn't buy it for me until I cleaned my whole room, corner to corner, separated belongings into new and old, and uncluttered each shelf. But then one day I came home, and all the new furniture was there anyway. I'd wanted a matching room the way I'd seen in magazines, and she'd wanted to surprise me. But by ninth grade, the rounded contours of the bed, the desk's cloudy pink knobs, it was all too young and feminine for me. I doodled on my headboard with Sharpie. I ripped a knob out and tossed it in the trash. I filled the drawers with crumpled paper. I hated the flowers, everywhere I looked.

I lived ten blocks from my high school, but I was always late. I'd finally get up when I had about fifteen minutes until first bell. I'd leave for school by passing as quickly as possible through the kitchen for a Pop-Tart and the living room to get to the front door. They were rooms that weren't mine anymore. I spent all my time in my room, with the wallpaper I picked at and the furniture I no longer loved.

One day after detention, I took the bus to the mall with three kids from my school. Chris, Matt, and Kyra had invited me to go with them. They were in detention because they'd left for lunch even though they weren't seniors, and I was there for always being late. We'd walked in and out of stores offering ear piercings and body glitter. We'd stopped in the food court, and when we passed the Japanese stand, Chris and Matt asked if the man handing out teriyaki chicken samples was my cousin, one of them holding his eyes at the corners. They stopped to buy some, and I went with Kyra to buy breaded chicken wraps with mayonnaise and watery tomatoes. "I don't even like teriyaki chicken," I'd murmured as we walked over, but I didn't think she heard. I was hot and embarrassed, and it didn't occur to me to tell them I wasn't Japanese, or that six people had already said that to me, or even to glare and walk away. All I ever did was smile weakly, laugh a little, and wait for the moment to pass, without making a big deal of it. The most important thing was for them to think I was a good sport about the whole thing. That was about all I knew.

When I got home, my mom was in the kitchen, making herself tea. "It's late," she said, as if she'd just remembered I was out. Her stomach stretched against her bathrobe so I could see the old shirt she wore underneath. She hadn't stopped working, but when she was home she was in bed, or in the bathroom, or rubbing her eyes and asking what I'd just said.

"I was at the mall," I said. Sometimes I lied about where I was, and I wondered if she thought I was lying now. I'd kept the cookie that had come with the sandwich I'd bought, and it was still in my purse—I could show it to her and prove I was telling the truth.

"Oh, that's nice," she said. She swirled the tea bag in her mug.

Is that your cousin? The words flared through my head. "Yeah, I ate there." I thought about telling her what he had said. But I didn't know how to start. I had never told her about anything that had happened before. There was one time I'd tried to, but her eyes had blinked back at me, blue and confused. "Why would they ask you if you could see well?" she'd said. "Do you need glasses?" I didn't know how to explain to her. All I knew was that kids said things to me, and I felt dark and shameful after, wrong for existing. How could I describe the feeling to someone who'd never had it before?

She took the tea bag out and put it in the trash. "I'm exhausted. Good night, sweetie." She kissed me on the forehead on her way out, and I flinched. I walked through the dining room and saw four library books stacked on the table. My mom never read anymore, so I stopped to touch them. The first one in the stack had a gold book club sticker on it and I looked at the due date: it was from last year. The following two novels were from the year before that. The last book in the stack was called *The Single Mother's Survival Guide*. I dropped the flap before I checked the due date; must have been years ago.

The next morning I took the books with me, and instead of going to school I walked to the library and dropped them in the slot outside. Then I turned around and went to school, about as late as I always was.

13
New York City, 2013

An uncomfortable part of moving in was being the help and receiving perks from other members of the help. It felt like betrayal at first, to accept things like warm, folded laundry and duvet covers left sharp and prim, but how quickly I acclimated to it all. The doormen signed for my packages and brought them to our floor. The housekeeper left my bathroom lemon-scented. Now I was someone who had a lobby I could stop into if I wanted to drop off extra bags when I was running errands. I was someone with a doorman, who held the door open for me when he saw me walking down the street, about to come home. I was someone who didn't wake up at footsteps or car exhaust or the slamming of a door. I didn't fear break-ins or burglaries or assault. I didn't wake up from nightmares at 2:00 AM and walk around checking all the cabinets and behind the shower curtain. I was now someone who felt insulated from those types of harm, someone who felt safe. I slept deeply.

*

"Did you *ever* take Mandarin, Willa?" Nathalie asked, her emphasis suggesting I might have studied and dropped it.

"I studied French in school," I said, and before she could ask for proof, "but I've lost a lot of it."

"But your dad—he speaks it, doesn't he?" Bijou leaned over her plate to look at me across the table. Gabe wasn't home, so it was the three of us at one end of the dining table, with Nathalie at the head.

"I don't really hear him speak it, but he does, yeah."

"Do you ever want to learn it to, you know, get more in touch with your culture?" Nathalie said, and I remembered how early on she had asked me if I spoke Mandarin. She'd told me how Bijou was studying Mandarin, and said it would have been nice if I could study with her, but she brushed it off, saying no matter, that wasn't important. I allowed a nod to her question; I did sometimes think of it, how I couldn't communicate with anyone in my dad's family except his sisters and his mother, who all spoke English.

"She told me she wanted to take it before, that she knows it's hard," Bijou told Nathalie. I tried not to glare at her.

"Is that true?" Nathalie neatly dipped a spoonful of rice into the curry she'd made.

"Maybe one day. When I have time." I looked down at my bowl, pushed the carrots around.

"Well, we have a proposition for you," Nathalie said. She and Bijou looked at me, their elbows on the table the same way.

I looked between them and said bluntly, "What?"

"We think you should go to class with Bijou. I already spoke to Li about it. She said two would be no problem, that you could help each other study."

"Well, wouldn't I be—way behind her?" I said, glancing quickly at Bijou. "I mean, she already knows so much."

"This is still Bee's first year. I thought you could go a few times by yourself. You won't be as caught up as Bijou, but she said it'll all even out in the lessons, it'll be fine. And we worked out a discount. So if you're interested, it would be about half the price each lesson."

"Oh, if she thinks it's going to be okay, then yeah—thank you," I said. "That sounds . . . great. What's half, well, what's the full price?" My thoughts rushed nervously, then giddily, and I felt like I wasn't supposed to mention money in front of Bijou. Was Nathalie offering to pay for them, or offering me a discount to pay for them myself?

"She's at a hundred an hour, so it would be fifty per lesson for you. I could take it out of your paychecks and pay her directly?" Nathalie offered.

It was more than I thought it would be, but I allowed myself to think, *Maybe this is a good idea.* Private language lessons were a luxury. What if I learned a lot, became fluent? What might that change for me? It was nice enough for Nathalie to procure a discount for me.

"Okay," I said. "Let's do it." They both smiled, and the conversation zoomed on from there. Later that night, Nathalie sent me a link to the textbook, saying, *Here's where you can buy your copy.* It was a hundred dollars, but a good thing to spend money on, right? I wouldn't tell my dad yet, I decided. Anyone could start Mandarin, pick up a language, put it down before being able to hold a conversation. I'd wait until I could say enough that he'd be impressed.

*

It felt strange to arrive without Bijou to Mrs. Zhang's. *Li*, I corrected myself in my head. Maybe I'd learn how to pronounce the word for teacher. My first lesson was while Bijou was at school, and I felt some relief at being able to go alone. Earlier that morning, Bijou had wished me good luck. I didn't like the thought of failing in front of Bijou: at least this would give me the chance to fail by myself. I knocked at the door, and I heard footsteps approach.

Li stood in the doorway, smiling so that I saw a dimple crease her right cheek. I felt shamed for thinking that she was severe and disapproving of me. Did I also think in stereotypes, the kind that people used when they thought about me? She had probably not thought anything about me at all.

"Welcome, Willa," she said. "It's nice to see you."

She led me past the narrow entryway and through a beige curtain. As the curtain closed, I tried to look out the dim gap, see what the rest of her home was like. But she'd set up the tutoring room in the front for that reason, I assumed, and there was nothing to glimpse but the corner of a refrigerator a room away. The tutoring room had a dusty, spartan feel to it. One round wooden table and two chairs with cushions were set up in the center. She gestured for me to sit.

"So," she said. "Are we starting from the beginning?"

I nodded, feeling apologetic. I had a tug of want for her to ask me about myself and my job, maybe ask if I liked nannying or what I wanted to do with my life. I'd tell her anything.

"No previous Mandarin?"

I shook my head. "I didn't grow up with my dad."

She looked up at my comment and then back at the textbook. I didn't know why I'd said that; it wasn't at all what she had asked, but usually when people asked me about speaking Mandarin, this was the answer they ended up needing to know. "You have the textbook?" Mine hadn't arrived yet, but Bijou had given me hers for the day.

Sunlight streamed through the window on the far wall and I looked at the beams of light, the dust suspended inside them. I coughed.

"Here," she said. "Some water." She pulled over a clear carafe and two stacked cups and poured me some. It had been sitting out, and it was lukewarm, but still, I drained the glass, trying to soothe my throat, the itch that seemed to rise from below my chest.

"This is strange, isn't it?" I said. She was smoothing down the pages of her textbook and looked up at me. I wondered how old she was; there were creases around certain spots, her eyes, the corners of her mouth, her forehead. Still, her face looked smooth and soft. She wore slippers and silky pants, a sweater that wrapped around her waist like a ballerina, tied in a bow near her left hip.

"What's strange?" she asked.

"That they sent me here. I mean, do you have any other nannies who do this?"

"Well, it made sense with Nathalie's plan," she said. "And to give Bijou someone to study with."

I nodded. "Right," I said, my instinct not to let her know I wasn't sure what she was talking about. There was a big, bare tree outside, its branches knocking against the window. I wondered what it looked like in the spring.

"So," she prompted. "Chapter one."

I looked back at the table and opened the textbook. I had never been a great student—first performatively, and then because it was too ingrained in me to discard. "Ready," I said. I had to remember to try.

*

Even though I still had six more solo lessons planned, Nathalie suggested that I tag along at Bijou's lessons in the meantime. "Just to observe, of course," she said, and I took that to mean that I wouldn't be paying for these. But I didn't know how to ask directly. They always spoke about money in these roundabout, euphemistic ways, and I listened carefully, trying to decipher the meaning.

"I mean, you're already there, so you may as well hear what they're going over. What are you going to do, sit outside in the hallway?" She laughed, and I did too, but while doing so I thought, *You know I do sit outside in the hallway usually, right?* Had she never wondered where I went during the lessons? I hadn't thought I was allowed to leave.

I didn't want to be embarrassed in front of Bijou, and on the walk over to our next lesson, my heart pattered darkly. To distract myself I asked her if she knew anything about Li.

"Like, does she have kids? Can you tell how old she is?"

"I know she's been tutoring Mandarin for ten or twenty years and used to be a college teacher," Bijou said. "Maybe she's like sixty."

"Bee, she's not sixty. How old do you think I am? Forty-five?"

We knocked at the door, and I smiled widely at Li, like, *Remember me, from that looooong hour we spent together last week?* We had not gotten far.

I was holding Bijou's shoulder in front of me as if she were a shield, and I gave her a little push to lead us down the hallway. There were photos all the way down of landscapes and tourist attractions, faded black-and-white photos of houses. But right where the curtain turned, I saw there was a smattering of family photos ahead. I ducked into the curtain. There were three chairs, three cushions, three cups stacked, and we sat down.

"Do you have kids?" I asked.

They looked at me sharply. Bijou leaned in and whispered to me, like Li couldn't hear, "*You're not allowed to speak English in here.*"

"Oh, well, I can't say that in Mandarin. I mean, I'm wondering. Before we start."

Li flipped her textbook open and pointed at the page number. "Willa, follow along. It'll help."

"I'm here to observe," I said.

"But you can also participate," she said and pointed again at the page.

"I didn't bring my textbook . . ." I trailed off.

Bijou flicked her eyes at me again, as if she couldn't believe what was happening. "You can share with me, I guess," she said, moving her chair over. I nodded and scraped my chair against the floor loudly as I inched to her side. I felt large, gangly, sitting next to Bijou, whose small body took up so little room, whose brain was absorbing information at a much faster rate.

At the end of the hour, we stood up and filed out. Bijou went first. As we exited the curtain, Li clucked her tongue and motioned in the opposite direction. She pointed to the first photo on the wall. It was her, young, with three kids by her side.

"My children," she said.

14

Kent, New York, 2005

I'd been at my dad's house for a little over a month when Cynthia announced they were going to dinner with Charlotte's godparents. "But it'll be several people you don't know. Maybe you'd rather stay here and relax?" I was relieved to be by myself for a night. My dad came home as they were fluttering around, Charlotte asking to borrow Cynthia's earrings, Esther hovering and then asking for whatever Charlotte got.

"I thought we could go for dinner," my dad said, his eyes on his feet as he pulled them out of his shoes. They didn't wear shoes in this house and kept them lined on racks in the entryway.

"Me and you?" We hadn't been alone together this whole time, and I felt as afraid of it as he must have. "Aren't you going to dinner?"

"Randall's not feeling well, so I thought the girls could go enjoy themselves and that you and I could go out on our own."

I followed my dad to the car. I wasn't *the girls.* I was something else. He turned music on loudly as he started to drive, so that when he spoke, he had to shout over it. "Do you like jazz?"

"I don't really know it," I shouted back.

"This is Charles Mingus," he said. I thought he was going to say more, but nothing came. It was a sad, soaring sound, sophisticated but melancholy, even as it sped up. I wondered what my dad heard in it. We pulled up onto a dark street. I caught the soft glow from orange lanterns skimming the front door.

"This is my favorite restaurant," he said as he turned off the ignition. "The girls hate coming here, though."

"I like it," I said immediately.

He took the keys out, spun them once in his palm. "I thought you might." I hopped out of the car, and he was on my side of the sidewalk, closing the door for me. When we reached the restaurant, he held the door open for me. I felt light walking in like that, prompted forward by kindnesses.

The restaurant was energetic and steamy inside, and a chorus of voices called out a greeting as we walked in. Conversation bounced off plates and cups that clattered as trays whipped through the air, balanced on the servers' open palms. The dark red carpet was stained by dirt and footprints, and I liked it, the imprint of all the other people who'd stood here and waited. He squeezed my shoulder and nudged me forward as he moved to the host. Tables dotted the center of the room, and bar seating lined each wall. The host led us to two barstools in the middle of the right wall, perched in front of a three-tiered bar with little lamps underneath the bottles.

Someone in an apron put two dripping glasses of ice water down. It was loud, louder than the car. There were couples with their heads together at the far end of the bar and large groups of men slamming down beers in the middle of the room. A server came over, and I heard my dad begin to order.

I felt a small relief, that I wouldn't have to look at the menu and ask what anything was.

Soon, they placed two beers and a little white vase in front of us, with two cups the size of shot glasses. I lifted my eyes to his face and saw he was carefully watching his hands as he poured us each a cup. I took in how large his hands looked, like baseball gloves, each finger broad and smooth. My hands were small, like a child's, much smaller than my mom's. Where did my undergrown hands come from? I took the cup when he handed it to me, and finally we met each other's eyes.

"Thanks," I said stiffly, though it wasn't the right thing to say. I pinched the skin on the back of my hand. I never said anything interesting; I never said anything right.

"We'll keep it between us," he said.

"Keep what?" It sounded clunky instead of conspiratorial. I closed my hand around the warm cup until my skin tingled, and then I poured the whole thing in my mouth. Right after, I saw him sip at his rather than take it as a shot, and I placed my cup back delicately. I picked up the bottle of beer by the neck, the way I'd seen older girls do at parties, and then placed it back down without drinking from it. I didn't want to seem overeager. Did he know I knew how to drink, that back home it was the only way I could blur myself into a group? I felt each second layering on top of the last like a game of Jenga; there was a limit, I knew, before everything would collapse.

"Charlotte—" I began. He was looking at the menu still; I guessed he had only ordered drinks. "Charlotte was showing me her photos yesterday." He turned to the server when he arrived and ordered swiftly, lengthily: silken tofu, sweet duck salad, o-toro sashimi, chicken hearts, beef tongue skewers, chicken livers—I turned from him and stopped listening. I'd eat anything.

"Have you ever tried tongue before?" he asked me. I'd heard his order, *beef tongue skewers*, but at the question I couldn't help but think of the word *tongue* over and over, something wet and pulsing. I wondered if he ever thought about whether I'd kissed someone or had a boyfriend. I felt embarrassed that I didn't, that no one would claim me in that ordinary way.

"No," I said quickly, when I'd been quiet for too long. "I haven't."

"It's my favorite," he said. "I think you'll like it."

"I will," I said. "I love Japanese food. All food." I felt dizzy, not from the beer or the warm sake but from a manic kind of focus, from being the center of his attention. I tried to think of something important to say, something to show him that I was interesting, discerning, valuable. I tried to remember the last time we were alone together, and I started to count in months. A plate was dropped off between us. What was something smart I could say?

"Do you know who Afong Moy is?" I asked him. The name pushed out from my brain like a shy but stubborn flower sprouting from cement. A girl in my school, Grace, had done a report on her when we were allowed to choose our own subject in history. She was the first Chinese woman to come to America. Grace was Chinese, but actually Chinese—two parents Chinese, second language Chinese, two months there every summer Chinese. My face felt warm in classes whenever we skipped over Asian history, when the teachers looked right at me, when the students turned and glanced. But that day, Grace stood and let everyone look at her. She mentioned the Chinese Exclusion Act, and that was the first time I'd heard of it. I wondered how many other things I didn't know. That was why I could never talk to Grace, never share a common ground. I scribbled the name *Afong Moy* in the margin of the notebook in front of me as she spoke, and tried to remember what she said clearly, so I could take notes as soon as no one could see me doing so. I'd clapped for her that day and thought of her often. But I had never spoken to her, and she had never spoken to me.

"Is that a singer?" He picked up his chopsticks and took something between them. It looked like the soft inside of a honeycomb, sliced up and slathered in sauce, spongy and textured.

I picked up a piece, too, right after him. "She's the first Chinese woman to come to America. She came in the 1800s, like 1830, but there's not any information on her. She was like a museum exhibit—people paid admission to come look at her, because she was Chinese. Then she was sold to P. T. Barnum, and then she disappeared. No one knows what happened to her." I didn't know if I was getting it right.

"Never heard of her," he said, but not in an interested way. The food between our chopsticks looked otherworldly, alive, with a thousand little crosses imprinted on its skin. "Tripe," he said. "My favorite."

"It's the tongue?" I asked. "Your favorite thing?"

"Oh, no, this is different, it's—"

Before he answered, I bit into mine. The waffling was soft, but the texture was chewy. I couldn't break it with my teeth, so I pushed the entire thing in my mouth, and I felt the ridges push up against my tongue.

"Cow stomach," he finished.

I licked my lips. My stomach flipped, with nerves and with novelty.

"The lining from the stomach actually," he said, eating another piece. The server came with two more small dishes: blistered shishito peppers, dark green and covered with thick flecks of salt, and a bowl of smooth tofu that looked like pudding, with a mess of sliced scallions on top. My dad held up the bottle of sake between two fingers and wagged it, and the server took it away to refill.

"What—what year did you and Nai Nai come here?" I said. "I know, like, the seventies, but . . ."

"It was 1971, 1972," he said. "Did Charlotte tell you that, about the woman? Poor girls, in school all summer, right? But at least I never made any of you sit through Chinese school every Sunday. My buddy makes his kids do that every weekend. They hate it."

I spooned the soft white tofu into my bowl. "Yeah," I said. I wondered if I should thank him. He took the serving spoon back from me and then shook scallions over my portion.

"Believe me, it was *not* fun growing up in New Jersey speaking Chinese," he said. "You wouldn't have wanted that."

I nodded, looking down. I believed him. I had a clear sliver of a memory from kindergarten, of thinking *Thank God I don't speak Chinese*, because everyone kept asking me if I could. I had said no with a sense of pride that I couldn't trace. What I meant was, *I'm American. I'm like you.* I bit into a shishito pepper; the skin fell off like rice paper, and a large fleck of salt smarted on my tongue.

"What was it like?" I mumbled.

He looked at me. "No walk in the park," he said. "Hey, remember how I used to take you to that sushi place off the highway? Hana?" The room became vivid to me when he mentioned it—the long wooden sushi bar, the white curtains that parted in the center, the way they wrote their specials each night in thick black marker on white strips of paper and hung them up with thumbtacks. The fake cherry blossom tree that stood next to the sink in the bathroom. I'd wash my hands and look at the pink tree and my reflection, feeling grown, chosen, special. We'd sit at the sushi bar, and they'd remember us each time, until it closed a few years ago. I ate like I'd been starved whenever I was with him, arriving home with my stomach stretched out, never any leftovers. He was proud of me when I ate robustly, when I finished everything he bought for me.

"And I'd get salmon rolls. Like three salmon rolls."

"And the tamago. Theirs was so sweet, but I think that's why you liked it."

I didn't like tamago, but I nodded. Maybe he was right. But I had never liked sweets—that was Charlotte.

Oyster shots arrived in double shot glasses, a single oyster floating on top of each like a drifting fetus. There was a dollop of something red on top, like cocktail sauce, and a fluorescent yellow egg yolk shifting like the inside of a lava lamp. A liquid, leaky yolk. I clinked glasses with my dad, and after I watched him throw his back, I did the same. A drop leaked out of my mouth, and I wiped it with my hand, checked to see if he noticed how I was sloppy, unrefined. I wasn't sure if I should swallow it all or chew it, and I held the slippery oyster between my teeth. Two perfect mounds of rice arrived in black bowls, next to a sizzling plate of breaded pork. Food kept arriving and disappearing. Sometimes my dad would narrate what it was. My taste buds were buzzing like living creatures. We must have talked a little bit, but I found myself not noticing if we did or didn't. I looked up at him from the side, saw the wrinkles that creased his forehead and near his eye, the corner of his mouth, though they were faint. His skin made me think of leather, not in the bad way people meant about beachgoers holding tinfoil to their chests, but of deep cognac-colored bags, the kind you ran your fingers over to feel. I wondered if I was staring at him like he was an exotic creature, the way people often did to me.

"Should we get anything else? Is there anything else you want?"

I shook my head and put my hand on my stomach, softly pushing out of my jeans. The plates weren't clean, but they were empty. I didn't feel embarrassed the way I so often did at the end of a meal, when I saw others' pizza crusts on the plates or pasta still coiled at the bottom of the bowl, while I'd finished my meal and the bread basket and drained my water glass until melted ice hit me in the teeth. I felt well-behaved, like a child, about to get a reward. I could still clean my plate.

"There's something else we can do, if you're up for it, if you're not tired," he said.

"I'm not." I waited as he signaled to the server, then paid the check with a stack of twenties from his wallet.

"This way," he said, motioning toward the back of the restaurant while he stood. I began to move to the front door despite that gesture—maybe he had to go to the restroom first—but he gently stopped me with his palm. He stepped in front of me and walked straight into the kitchen, gave a short nod to some of the cooks, who nodded back, and then took a sharp right down a darkened hallway.

"Dad?" The word still felt dusty inside my mouth.

He turned around for a second, tilting his head over his shoulder. It wasn't so much a smile as a look in his eye, a look that made me think of him being young and mischievous, sneaking off down an alley. It was a glimpse of him I had never seen, and it reminded me that there must be thousands of these—parts of him I didn't know. What if we hadn't missed so many years—what would I know about him if he'd stayed? He paused, waiting for me to catch up. I skipped the last few steps and grabbed on to him above his elbow. His arm felt thick with muscle, warm inside his shirt. There was one light bulb hanging at the end of the hallway and what looked like a dark, tumbling stairwell ahead of it.

He motioned for me to enter first. I'd never said no to my dad, and tonight wouldn't be the night I began, not when things were going so well. I stepped into the dark. The staircase spiraled down, and as I held on to it, I felt the paint flake off the iron. I lifted my hand up and saw a flicker of black stuck to the inside of my knuckle. The music cascaded up under my feet: deep twirls of saxophone, the tinkling of piano, a ritzy tapping of drums. It was dim, the carpet dark and soft under my shoes. The booths were red leather, miniature, made for one person on each side. There were small candles in little shot glasses everywhere, and the servers were wearing vests and bow ties, curlicue mustaches jaunty underneath their noses. A giant quivering chandelier hung above the bar, spinning what little light was in the room off its hanging glass.

"My hidden gem," my dad said, and I turned to him. "For special occasions."

He held up two fingers and we were shuttled to a table. He told me I could pick anything I wanted, the way he used to when I was young and it was his weekend and we went to a restaurant or a toy store. It made me feel precious but came with the pressure to take hold of as much as I could, as if it were my last chance. He didn't say goodbye when he left for the first time. My mom said I walked around the house for days, asking where he was. I don't think it was his fault, leaving—they were careful not to tell me why they split, but I remembered my mom, her whispered apologies into the phone at night. How she walked around like someone caught, not left.

I looked at the menu, and I thought, *He'd never let Charlotte or Esther have a drink here, even when they turn my age.* And it hurt me rather than buoyed me, that he would always keep them safe, but that I was expected to watch out for myself. For a second I was about to say I wouldn't have anything. But then the bartender came, and my dad ordered an old-fashioned, and I pointed to something on the menu. Maybe it was my last chance.

My dad leaned in over the table. The tablecloths were white and starched. "You're okay, aren't you, Willa?"

I coiled back into my seat, uncertain what he meant. "I'm okay," I said slowly.

"I mean, you don't need anything, do you? You know—you could ask me for anything you need."

I had already had a beer and three warm cups of sake. My mind spun. What could it be? I needed—a spot at a table, somewhere. I needed a throat that could ask for things. I needed a picture of me and both of my parents, taped on my wall like it wasn't important enough to frame. I needed someone to teach me how to drive. I needed somewhere to go where I didn't have to think about each sentence before I said it. The drinks had made me feel open, but the food had made me sleepy, and my thoughts ran into each other lifelessly, deflated. He'd ask again. I would prepare, so that next time he asked, I knew what to say. The cocktails landed in front of us, and he held his out to knock against mine. "I know," I said. "I'm fine."

"You know, everyone has trouble when they're young. I don't worry about you," he said, settling back against his seat and straightening out his sleeves. "I worry about Esther, you know, she's so scared of everything, she needs help for everything, she always has. And Charlotte is so picky, you know, I worry about that, being too particular. But you never were like that, picky, or afraid. I know you can handle life. You're tough."

I wondered why he thought that. And why had my mom sent me here? It was more than her baby, who had been there for months. Maybe because I spoke of my dad like he was a knight on leave—as soon as he was done slaying a dragon, he'd come save me. Like he'd never done anything wrong in his life, except leave me there. Like he hadn't left me there, to start his real family. When I thought of it that way, I felt a sad warmth for my mom—I guessed she deserved that as much as he did. He was so nice to his daughters, but I was no longer clay. I wasn't soft between his hands, ready to mold in his image. I wondered if whatever structure I'd picked up along the way repelled him. Did it remind him of my mom? Or maybe it reminded him of a version of himself, the one he used to be with her.

"I've never told any of the girls about this place," he said. "So. It's our secret." He flicked his palm, the gesture vague but the meaning precise: the sake, the beer, the cocktails, the two of us. We'd go home and I'd feel quiet and the door would be closed and when I walked behind him I wouldn't be able to grab on to his arm. Sometimes when I sat across from him quietly, or when I was in the kitchen when he came home from work and I couldn't think of anything to say, this taut feeling stretched my chest, and I thought to myself: *Time is almost up, and then that's it. That's your whole chance.* Would it be just tonight, the two of us in a secret snow globe that was down a stairwell of a restaurant his family wouldn't go to? In a way, I was happy to be hidden; that what he'd shown me belonged to only the two of us.

We drove home in silence, the music back on, but this time the silence felt comfortable, like if I wanted to, I could reach over and turn the volume down and say something. The windows were dark when we got home, so I thought everyone would be asleep and that we could creep inside and I could lie down and that would be the last thing I remembered, this feeling of a balloon filled and floating. But as we pulled into the driveway, another car followed us, and we all opened the doors at the same time.

"Perfect timing," my dad said brightly. The girls folded themselves out of the back seat; they must have slept on the ride home. He held out his arms and they each attached themselves to one side. I clutched at my elbows, sick with how simple it was: there was no room for me there.

"How was Montero's?" Cynthia said, leaning over to kiss him on the cheek.

"Delicious, like always," he said. I thought maybe he'd turn and wink at me or make some sort of subtle gesture, to let me know we were still carrying a secret between us. I looked at the back of his head. For once, I knew what I wanted.

15

New York City, 2013

Bijou and I were going to be left alone in the house for three days while Nathalie went to a conference in Florida and Gabe drove upstate to see his parents. The dates overlapped and no one seemed to think much of leaving us there, though it would be the first time.

"Will it be cold up there?" I asked Gabe, the night before they left.

"Last time I was there at this time, it was twenty below," he said. "But my parents like it better when I come in the winter because that's when the second-house people—the tourists—they all go away, and the town's quiet again."

Bijou and I were making rice bowls with asparagus and bok choy and neat rectangles of tofu, a poached egg nestled on top.

"It's the best in the summer," Bijou said.

Gabe nodded. "Canoeing and hiking and swimming. But my parents are always working. My sister is always working. Moneymaking season, everyone is busy."

I portioned out four bowls, leaving one to the side for Nathalie, who would be home soon. I put Bijou's in front of the middle seat at the counter, so we would sit on either side of her. Gabe didn't eat dinner with us often. He would eat at odd hours, whenever he felt like it, would scoop something into a bowl and put headphones in or take it down his hallway. I'd heard Nathalie scold him for this—"We'll eat together in an hour!" He'd take out an earbud, eyes wide and innocent. "Nat, I'm hungry now."

"Your parents—do they ever come here for the holidays?" I felt a pressure to be speaking, as if I were the entertainment.

"They're terrified of the city," Gabe said. "They'll come every few years. My youngest sister—the favorite—she still lives twenty minutes away from them. My mom reminds me every time she calls."

I pulled out a bottle of hot sauce from the cabinet before sitting down. I'd never heard of this brand before, but I'd gotten in the habit of shaking it over everything I ate.

"Aha!" Gabe said. "I thought you'd been dipping into my hot sauce."

I froze with the bottle in my left hand. "This is yours? I'm sorry, I can use the other one."

"No, I'm only joking! Isn't it the best?"

I closed the cabinet and brought it back to my seat. "Where did you find it?"

"I worked at a medical clinic in Belize years ago, and this is all anyone uses over there."

I tried to place Belize on a map in my head. "Have you done that a lot? Gone to—work abroad?" I had so little idea what Gabe did for a living—doctor, yes, but what kind of doctor, there were so many—that it was awkward to talk to him. It felt too late to ask for those details now, and it had felt too forward to ask for them then.

"Mmm, it wasn't exactly work, more of a volunteer placement. I did three months in Belize, one month in Guatemala, three months in South Africa, and one in Nigeria."

"Octavia's mom is from South Africa," Bijou said. "They're going there next month."

"Our winter is their summer in South Africa," he said. "It's the best time."

"I know that," Bijou said.

"Oh, excuse me." He stole a piece of bok choy from her bowl even though he had plenty. "Maybe we'll go sometime."

"It's fun at Grandma's, even when it's not summer," Bijou said. "I wish I could come with you."

"But you don't want to miss school. And the apples aren't ready to pick," Gabe responded. "Her favorite thing to do there. Mine, too, when I was younger. We never get to go anymore because Bijou has so many activities during picking season. When I was younger, me and my brother, we'd roam those orchards for hours. Climbing trees and picking apples and using them as baseballs in the field." He cut a piece of tofu with the side of his fork. "We'd run out in the morning and come back when the sun went down. *No* worries whatsoever."

"Sounds nice," I said.

"Sounds kind of boring to sit in an apple tree all day," Bijou said.

He smiled. "You know, I think I would be bored by it now. But I wasn't then." He looked at me. "God, don't I sound old? I bet your parents say the same types of things to you, Willa. We all believe that our youth was the most pure, the ideal."

I smiled faintly, swallowing the sourness in the back of my throat. I thought about what my dad might have been doing as Gabe was tossing an apple in his hand, lying back in sun-stiffened grass. How did they get visas then, what did he pack to move across the world? The immigration quotas from the Exclusion Act had been lifted only six or seven years before, meaning that the possibility of the move must have felt uncharted, new, scary. Or maybe he was too young to feel those things; maybe he wasn't scared until he got here, to an unfriendly country where he didn't know how to order lunch. Someone must have sponsored them, but I didn't know who. Did he miss his friends, his house? Did he tell his mom he didn't want to go? Gabe took another bite, and after he swallowed, he hummed to himself dumbly, twirling his fork and scattering rice on the counter. He didn't move to wipe it up but took another bite.

My dad wouldn't talk about his childhood, or he'd put it too far away, but it was like I could feel it still, like he had passed it down to me. Maybe you could do that with sadness, the same way you could with carefreeness. Sometimes I felt the weight of something larger than me, as if it had slithered into my bloodstream, as if it had passed down a heaviness hanging somewhere behind my eyes. Gabe finished eating and stood up to place his bowl in the sink. I took his discarded napkin and swept the rice he'd dropped onto the floor.

*

On the last night that Gabe and Nathalie were gone, I watched television in the living room. Two episodes of *Friends*, where they sat on a couch in a coffee shop, then on a couch in their apartment, then around a kitchen table. I flipped to *Sex and the City*, and the women gathered in a diner, then at a bar, then on the sidewalk while Carrie smoked a cigarette. My eyes burned; I hadn't been watching much TV lately. I got up and walked over to Bijou's room, pushing the already ajar door open a few inches farther. Her blonde hair fanned out on the pillow and she was on her side, clutching a stuffed elephant. Once she'd told me Gabe had brought it back from Africa.

I walked back into the living room and hesitated for the shortest side of a second before walking into their room. I walked through the closet into the bedroom and slid the light switch up only halfway, so the room was bathed in a soft, gentle light. The bed was neatly made with square corners like mine, flanked by matching dark teak nightstands with a lamp on each side. His and hers. No TV, but there was a silver laptop on what looked like Gabe's side.

I'd been into their bedroom once before with Bijou, but I hadn't seen the bathroom. I slid the door open to a cavernous black-tiled cube, almost as big as my bedroom. There were matching white sinks in front of a mirror that stretched over one wall, a tub like a small swimming pool, and a separate shower behind a glass door, but the rest of the room was covered in inky-black square tiles, each one half a foot across. The toilet was behind its own door, sectioned off, the way I'd once seen in a hotel. A Lucite vanity table stood along one wall with a matching clear chair in front. The chair scraped the floor and echoed; I froze for a second, listening to the sound fade away.

I had such dark circles; they sat under my eyes like the smudged shadows of two moons. I splashed water on my face and squeezed some of Nathalie's face wash onto my hands and then onto my face in slow, circular motions. I dried off on a white towel hanging next to the sink, then sat back down. I picked up jars and tubes, reading the labels, though many were in different languages: French, Korean, Japanese. I sprayed a mist onto my face that smelled like rose petals. I tipped a tall clear bottle of toner onto a cotton ball and rubbed it over my forehead and nose and neck. When I pulled it away, the cotton was dark, even though I wasn't wearing makeup.

I chose the most ornate jar of moisturizer, a container jagged like a diamond, and smoothed it everywhere, even my hands. Then I took another scoop and massaged it into my chest. I felt my heart beating quickly. There was makeup left behind too: a few gold tubes of lipstick, a cream blush, powdered bronzer, and a half-used foundation. I picked up an eyebrow pencil and outlined the shape of my brows. It made me look older but in a way that I liked. I picked up one of the lipsticks and put it to my lips. The stick was red, but the color came out subtle, natural, like I'd bitten down and my lips had filled with blood. My skin had a pearly sheen. I turned my head from side to side. I looked better like this. I put everything back the way it was and went back down my hallway. The next morning, I admired how undisturbed everything still looked, as if I'd never been there at all.

*

While waiting outside activities for Bijou, I wrote notes to my parents explaining why I wasn't going to come home for

Christmas. I'd open up the notepad of my cell phone and think of how to explain. I thought about what I'd write if I could actually be honest.

Dad, last year, you guys had a family over I didn't even know and you sat me on the side of the table with them, and I spent hours with them and barely any time with you. My dad at the head of the table, a gracious host I barely knew.

Hi Mom, I wish I could come home, but why can't I see you—why does it have to be with him? I thought of the things we did when it was the two of us—the gardens, the picnic blankets, the pancakes. If there was a holiday that included those.

I alternated holidays, so my absence was as regular as my presence. I imagined them all talking about me at their two separate holidays, how uncomfortable I was, how I ate too much and how I didn't have good manners and how I was never able to seamlessly join the conversation. How glad they were that I wasn't there.

I have to work on Christmas, I wrote to them in the end. *But it'll be kind of fun. They're having a party. It will still be like a holiday.*

16

Durland, New Jersey, 2001

When I was younger, my mom traded in the sedan my dad bought her for a blue pickup truck she bought used. I had never seen a mom drive a pickup truck before. It was the metallic blue of nail polish or eye shadow; later, it would occur to me that it was a strange color choice for her, someone who shrank out in the open as if wishing for a column to stand behind. I didn't find it embarrassing until middle school, and by that time she was dating Ray and they traded it in again for a sedan. But she liked the pickup truck, and so did I. In the old sedan, she would pick me up from school with so many plants in the back seat I would squeeze in next to them, leaves grazing my cheeks and shoulders and seat belt. With the pickup truck, everything had its place in the back—bags of mulch, sand, compost, manure, the starts of little trees, a cooler for our lunches, picnic blankets. Everything she needed for her garden, and our escape days.

Escape days: when she'd come into my room and stroke my hair awake before waiting for me in the kitchen. I was supposed to go to school, but she'd say we should go on an adventure instead. She usually wanted to go to a garden or an outdoor park, to look at flowers or put our bare feet in grass. Sometimes the beach, sometimes the city for a museum. "We deserve a little escape, don't you think?" I'd nod, because I felt like I should, and drink the juice she'd poured for me even with just-brushed teeth. She had thermoses of hot chocolate and large water bottles, sandwich bags of cucumbers sliced and steeped in sugar and vinegar, hard-boiled eggs we'd dip in soy sauce, and white bread lined with liverwurst, which I stopped admitting to liking by age ten. I would remind her to call my school before we left. The school would call as soon as I didn't show up, and if my mom wasn't there to tell them that I was sick, they might think I had gone missing.

"But today is the spelling test," I told her in a small voice. There was a spelling bee every year, and the qualifying test was in English class. I was good at spelling, and the year before I'd been sick with the flu on the qualifying day. I'd said it tentatively, and I already knew I shouldn't.

"The what?" Her hair was getting oily near the roots, strands sticking to her forehead.

"The spelling test," I said. I held my elbow in one hand. My mom looked from me to the dining room table, where she'd already laid out cut sandwiches and bags of fruit, a rolled-up picnic blanket, a bottle of sunblock. Most weeks she couldn't remember to pack me lunch, but now, all of this.

"Right," she said, reaching a hand up to drag through her hair. I imagined her fingertips coming back shiny, moist. "Right. I must have missed that on the calendar."

I couldn't help looking at the pile of mail on the counter, where the school calendar lay unopened.

"It's, is it Thursday?" I asked, yawning.

"Wednesday, sweetie."

I tugged on the sleeve of her bathrobe. "The tests are Thursday!" She looked down at me, and I saw her eyes were bloodshot, full. "I thought it was Thursday today," I said.

She pulled me into her stomach, my head pushing up against her softness, and she squeezed me until her breath steadied. Then she pulled away, and I went to get dressed. I didn't tell her to call the school, because I didn't want them to say anything about the spelling test. Maybe if I had gone missing, they'd let me retake it.

The next day, she was in the kitchen in her bathrobe when I came downstairs. "Spelling bee day!" she squealed. Sometimes my mom was like a kid; it made me feel wizened and old. She believed any outrageous thing anyone told her, still wrote *Santa Claus* on my Christmas presents, gasped happily if a ladybug landed on her arm. Even when I was young, I noticed this. I looked at the kitchen counters, wondering if she'd packed me lunch today. But they were still cluttered with yesterday's remnants, a chef's knife lying askew on a cutting board, torn-off lettuce wilting near the sink.

"Spelling bee day," I repeated. Did she remember this was the qualifying test, that the spelling bee wasn't for a month?

"Good luck, sweetie," she said, kissing me on the top of the head. "Win me something, won't you?"

I told her I'd try, but I didn't explain more. I knew they wouldn't redo a whole test for me, just because I had spent the day sitting in grass with her, tearing crust from bread. When I got to school, I didn't say a word.

17

New York City, 2013

It had been snowing on and off for weeks. Mountains of dishwater snow piled up on street corners and leaked gray-brown puddles into crosswalks. There were tourists everywhere, walking too slowly and stopping too often to take pictures and taking forever to order coffee. I liked red bows and twinkly lights wrapped around tree trunks as much as anyone, but it wasn't enough to make up for the rest of December in Manhattan. The days passed in a mute haze of cold so deep that it stung my skin as I walked to and from Bijou's activities day after day.

"So you'll be with your mom on Christmas Eve and me on Christmas," the man across from us on the subway said to his daughter. He was wearing a green beanie and a puffy jacket, looking down at his hands as he spoke to her. She looked straight ahead but not at us. "You'll get two Christmases."

The little girl looked up at him and said something into his shoulder.

"Well, Christmas Eve is when your mom's family celebrates Christmas," he said. Then with a start, he added, "I mean, we're all still a family, you know what I mean." He reached up and rubbed at his neck.

I noticed that Bijou was also listening, staring at a space on the girl's lap. How did two Christmases and two sets of presents sound to her? We came to the next stop and a new wave of kids flooded in.

On Christmas Eve, the Adriens were having a dinner at their apartment that they had invited me to. On Christmas Day, they were driving upstate to see Gabe's family. I would have two Christmases again: one with them, and one by myself. I was trying something out—being alone, opting out of the family celebrations where I never felt like family. I spent most of the holidays on edge, suspecting that they didn't want me there. We got off at the next stop, and I kneaded my fingers into my chest, as if I could pierce bones through skin straight to the muscle underneath.

*

We whirred through Thursday afternoons with Mandarin lessons and phrase-book conversations that were more revealing than the exchanges we had on our own. Bijou had to ask me where I was born, how old I was, and what sports I had played in high school. I had to ask her the same questions, but I already knew all the answers for her. When I answered, I was giving her new information, like that I had three siblings.

"I thought you had two sisters?"

I'd told her that only once. "I also have a brother, a half brother. My mom's."

Li clucked her tongue at my English. I pointed at Bijou. "You saw it was her, right?"

After class, Bijou asked to see a photo of my brother too. "He's much younger," I said. "I'd have to look."

I imagined we'd go on like this for months, drawing characters together at the kitchen table, turning over flashcards, painstakingly telling each other our birthdays and laboring over how to say the birth year. But one month into the lessons, Nathalie forwarded me an email, with her own message on top.

Just in from Stanton: Mandarin starting next semester! So we're going to be canceling our lessons with Li. Of course, you can continue to see her on your own if you'd like, outside of work hours.

And that was that. I put my hundred-dollar textbook underneath my bed. I'd go back someday. When I had time. Every so often I opened the notebook again, where I'd written down the small sentences I'd learned to say in another language: *My name is Willa Chen. I have five people in my family: my dad, my mom, my younger sisters, and my younger brother. I'm American.* Things I'd been saying my whole life, things I still couldn't say.

*

There were times I went out with friends—old coworkers, old classmates. When Renata invited me to her art opening, I told myself I should go. I had gone to one of her shows a couple of years ago, and it had been fun; we'd been working together at a bar then. The last gallery had been in Bushwick, twelve empty industrial streets past the subway, but this one was in Chelsea, within stepping distance of actual, impressive museums. My first instinct was not to go, but didn't I think sometimes about how I wanted friends? So I went. The gallery show started about an hour after I was done working

It was a bright, empty space with Renata's giant oil paintings stretching down the walls. They were vibrant, expressive portraits, set on the subway, on a street corner, on a black folding chair in Madison Square Park. Everyone was drinking champagne out of triangular flutes—women in loose dresses and architectural heels, men in tailored suits. And me. I drained one fizzy glass while I looked around. I thought for an improbable second, *What if Gabe or Nathalie ended up showing up?* I didn't know what plans either of them had tonight. Only Nathalie had been home when I'd left, and sometimes they went out without each other while one of them stayed home with Bijou. What if they saw me here, mingling with friends, having my own life, having my own life somewhere important? My shoulders lifted with the idea. I saw Renata across the room and tried not to hover around her, wanting like everyone else to stake a claim to the person whose show it was. She saw me and waved but was swept up in a crowd; fifteen minutes later, she found me, descended on me with a hug and an air-kiss, asked me to tell her what was new.

"I'm nannying now," I said, "living in Tribeca." I had a flash of Renata trying to help me figure out what else I wanted to do after work one night, over whiskey-gingers at the bar that stayed open later than ours. She had first wanted to be a poet, then became a visual artist. I had loosely wanted to try acting but didn't anymore—maybe I should try writing? sculpture? ceramics? What did we land on? Did we decide? "Thinking about grad school," I added vaguely.

"Oh, that's *great*, Willa, that'd be so great for you—" she said earnestly, but then someone else grabbed her elbow—"Can I introduce you to someone?"—and tugged her away, and she squeezed my forearm twice before disappearing. I wondered if any of our other coworkers were here. We used to stay out so late that I often walked into my apartment as the sun was rising. Wouldn't it be fun to do that one more time? I walked around the gallery four times, wondering if someone might talk to me. When no one did, I walked back out. I was home before ten.

18

New York City, 2013

The day before Christmas Eve, the elevator opened and James had his arms full of hydrangeas. He transferred them to mine, delicately, and I held the bouquets like they were babies. I thanked him softly as Nathalie came out.

"There they are," she said. "I wanted them delivered tomorrow, but the florists were booked weeks ago for holiday delivery. Let's hope these hold up." She came over to me and leaned in, inspecting them.

"I've never seen red hydrangeas before," I said.

"Yes, hydrangeas, how did you know? Red ones are hard to find, sometimes. I thought they'd be Christmasy, but I'm actually partial to the white ones here." She picked at the bottom bouquet in my arms and I shifted it, hoping to give her a better look. "Though this one looks almost wilted! They better survive until tomorrow."

She touched a few of the petals roughly, and without thinking I pulled my arms slightly away, like she was too close to the doll I was cradling. "I'll put them in water for you if you want?" I offered.

"That'd be great, Willa," she said, tightening her ponytail and walking off. "Use the square vases—third shelf. When you're done, I'll sprinkle them around."

In the kitchen, I filled up the teakettle and put it on the stove. I laid the three bouquets out in front of me on the kitchen island, two white and one red. Hydrangeas were so round and full, like pom-poms or the frosted part of cupcakes. I took them out of their paper bundling and untied the strings holding them together, spreading them out in front of me like vegetables I needed to dice. I snipped off the bottom of each one at an angle, the insides of their stems dripping out tender and pale. On my tiptoes I inched out the square vases and filled them with cold water from the sink. When the water boiled, I poured it into a wide, shallow bowl and dipped the stems in. After half a minute, they went in their vases. I cleaned up the trimmings, the paper and plastic left over from the bouquets, the bowl I'd used for the hot water. I left the vases on the kitchen island. I hoped that trick, learned years ago, still worked. I'd done it with great care but felt embarrassed about it, glad no one had seen my little ritual. I walked back down my hallway as I saw James come back up to drop off a dry-cleaning delivery for Nathalie. I smiled at him in a way I hoped he understood, meaning something like, *does it ever end with them?* Even though sometimes I wished it never would. I went back to my room and wondered what Nathalie would wear tomorrow as I looked through the clothes I owned. The room had a large, deep closet that my things couldn't fill. The closets at my last apartments had been so small and shallow that I'd thrown things out to make space. I saw their absences like phantom limbs, that dress that I'd sold at a thrift store, that turtleneck sweater I'd let Lucy keep. I didn't have an elegant yet casual winter dress to pull on, but I wasn't working today and there was a row of stores nearby.

A blonde salesgirl in a camel-colored hat greeted me as I walked into one. "Hi there!" she chirped. "Do you need help finding anything?"

I began to sort through the nearest rack. "I'm looking for something to wear to dinner tomorrow." I was getting so unused to talking to new people that exchanging a few words with the salesperson made me nervous.

"Is it something fancy?" she asked, getting up from behind her desk, and I shook my head. "Do you live in the neighborhood?"

I looked at the fabric of the dresses I was pushing apart. "Mm-hmm," I said. "Over on Watts." I felt a tinge of smugness. I knew that there was an image it provided that wasn't true. If I were this young and living on Watts Street, then I could afford anything in the store; the buttery-soft leather jacket I'd touched, the floor-length alpaca sweater hanging in the window.

I picked out a dress and held it out in front of me. "Can I try this on?"

"We put those on sale because we're getting a newer shipment in next week, but it's such a steal," the salesgirl said as she led me to the dressing room. "I love the collar."

I tried it on behind a velvet curtain. It was a wine-colored red dress with sleeves to my wrists and exaggerated cream triangles for a collar, with a flared skirt that fell a couple of inches above my knees. I looked young in it, like a girl, but in a way I thought proved that I wasn't one, that I was an adult playing dress-up. I paid for it with my debit card and walked another loop around the neighborhood, the dark purple bag hanging from my wrist like a sign.

I headed up the elevator with my new dress, and when the doors opened, I was met with a clatter of voices. Nathalie's sister lived in Connecticut. Every so often, her kids would appear in the apartment. "They came in to see their allergist, and Lillian dropped them here for a few hours to see Bijou," Nathalie would say, something flippant and annoying like that, and I would have three children staring up at me.

"Willa!" Nathalie cried. "Oh, thank God you're back—do you mind? Lillian and Ben were just here. They're going to Ben's family's tonight uptown, and I didn't know they'd be here today. They asked if we could watch Noah and Luke for a couple hours, but I have to run out for this coffee date, and Lillian will come back to get them soon. Last-minute gift emergency, she said." She had her shoes on and her coat tied around her waist, and as she spoke to me, she walked past me to the elevator, her finger hovering above the button. "Do you need me to stay?"

I shook my head. She punched the elevator button. "Ooh, I love that shop," she said, pointing at my shopping bag as the doors closed. What had just happened? I wasn't even supposed to be working today.

Noah and Luke were eight and nine, and I couldn't tell them apart. They were scrawny, with a weaselly look about them. The last time they were here, they'd held their eyes with their fingers and told me they were Chinese too. We'd all been sitting down to dinner. "*Boys*," Lillian had said; then the dinner proceeded awkwardly and it was not brought up again.

"Well, let's watch a movie?" I suggested.

*

I had been trying to get Nathalie alone ever since Lillian had left the day before. Finally, a couple of hours before the Christmas Eve dinner, I walked into the kitchen while she was walking out.

"Nathalie," I said. "I've been meaning to tell you. Something happened when Noah and Luke were here. They were being, um, they weren't listening to me."

Nathalie glanced at her slim silver watch. "They never listen, do they?"

"Yeah, well, I was trying to clean up the living room, they'd thrown the pillows everywhere while watching a movie. They, well I guess it was Noah, not Luke—Noah, he slapped my butt as I was passing him, and I thought it was inappropriate." Saying the word *butt* to Nathalie seemed so juvenile, it was almost offensive. I'd gone over my word choice before, but there seemed to be no better option.

She blinked once. "Oh, I'm sure he didn't mean anything by it, but I'll be sure to tell Lillian that it's not acceptable for him to touch *anyone* like that, *not* good behavior." She lowered her voice. "Lillian can be a bit of a laissez-faire parent. Once Luke pulled on Bijou's sleeve so hard that it almost ripped! I mean, it only stretched out her shirt, but still, Bijou was upset. I didn't have them over for months afterward." Nathalie shook her head and straightened her own sleeves. "Lillian was always a bit self-absorbed. Well, thanks for telling me, Willa, I'll pass it along, and so sorry you had to deal with them acting up. Thank goodness Bijou is such an angel, I always think." She reached out and patted me on the arm, and then turned and went back into the kitchen, even though she had been leaving before. I felt as if I had been dismissed, and I gathered my scarf and my hat and my jacket and got in the elevator.

At the coffee shop across the street, I sat down and held my hands against my round mug. *At least I told her*, I thought. *I mean, they are only nine, so I guess it was, like, a kid thing.* I didn't know why I had told Nathalie, what I had expected her to do.

We had been watching a movie I'd seen with Bijou ten times before. I had my trick for watching movies when Bijou had friends over. They got annoyed if I wouldn't sit through the entire thing, so I'd watch with them for the first half hour—that's what it took for them to be sedated by the screen. Then I'd creep up, go to the kitchen, get myself something to drink or snack on, and sit back down at the dining room table, where I could scroll on my phone in peace—I could still see them from there, but they couldn't see me without turning their heads. That day, I eased myself up, and Luke asked if I could get him some juice. *Fine*, I thought. "Orange or apple?" I'd even asked, like such a good babysitter. Noah asked for some too. I brought them two cups of apple juice and set them down on the coffee table. "You're blocking the screen!" they had yelled. "Um, you're welcome for the juice," I'd said. I sat back at the table. The heat was too high. I crossed behind the couch to turn the heat down; the panel was by the elevator. And when I crossed back behind the couch to return to the dining room, Noah had whipped his head around and slapped my behind. He'd grinned up at me devilishly after. "Sit down and watch the movie," he said. "You're missing it." I was embarrassed to remember the way he said it, his certainty, his anger—he wasn't even ten, and somehow, I felt scared.

*

After finishing my coffee, I crept back into the elevator and hid in my bedroom until dinner. I felt like I was the one who'd done something wrong, like I needed to avoid Nathalie. I waited on my bed until I heard the elevator come up, and then I closed the last button on the nape of my neck and walked out.

"Oh, don't you look nice. I love that dress," Nathalie said as she turned around. "Willa, this is Gabe's sister Deirdre and her husband, Paul; you two, this is Willa."

"And this is Tommy," Deirdre said, pulling a teenager over. His hair was buzzed and dirty blond, so that it flickered when the light hit but looked dull in the shadows. I could see the outline of the skull T-shirt he had on under his ironed blue button-down. Bijou came up behind me and said hi to him and pulled me away, a little more forcefully than necessary.

"Um, *ouch*," I said to her, tugging my elbow back.

"Mom didn't make any welcome drinks," she said.

"So this is an emergency."

Bijou gave me a withering look. "Wow, lipstick," she said, crossing her arms.

I motioned for her to keep walking. "Okay, okay."

"Nana used to make a welcome drink at Christmas."

"Well, is she coming?" I asked.

Bijou looked at me. "Nana? She died two years ago."

"Oh, I'm sorry," I said, my face hot. How had I not grasped that when they spoke of her, it was in the past tense?

"So we need to make them," she said, leading me to the kitchen.

The french doors of the kitchen were closed, and inside the air was steamy and fragrant. "What's your mom making for dinner?" I asked. "Turkey or ham or something?"

"Pork tenderloin. That lipstick is really dark," she said. "But I like how serious you look." I touched my index finger to my bottom lip.

She threw open the fridge and began to rearrange things. I slid onto a stool and watched, leaning my chin in my hand. The kitchen felt too occupied to move around in: three of the four burners were being used, the oven was full, there were cutting boards and knives strewn about. I started to clear whatever was around me, a slotted spoon and a spatula and Nathalie's coffee mug—inside the mug, a last sip of red wine. Bijou put a carton of apple cider in front of me.

"Let's heat that up and put cinnamon sticks inside, like little straws."

I obeyed. I pulled out a silver saucepan; she poured the cider inside. I turned on the last burner and she motioned for me to pull down the mugs, not the everyday mugs but the matching porcelain ones with curlicue letter *A*s. I put them on the counter where she could reach, and she motioned for me to stir the cider while she arranged them on two trays. She got on her knees and dug her hands into the cabinet and emerged with a box of cinnamon sticks. One went in each mug, and two to swirl in the cider. She stuck a pinky into the pot and motioned for me to pour the steaming liquid. Bijou hovered with a dish towel. Only when I was sure I hadn't spilled did I glare at her for her stance.

"What's all this?" Nathalie asked, closing the french doors behind her, reaching for the apron on the counter.

Bijou was arranging the cinnamon sticks so that they all fell to the same angle, and she didn't answer.

"Welcome drinks?" I said.

"Mm, really, Bee. Welcome drinks. Okay, that's sweet. Everyone will like that. Can you finish up?"

"Mom, look, we're done." Bijou picked up one tray and handed it to me. Holding the tray, I felt exquisitely like help, a clarifying moment as I stood there in my lace-collar dress. Nathalie motioned to the table with her chin. "You can put it over there, Willa," she said, and walked out.

"Well, look who's finally decided to join us," I heard Nathalie say as her brother arrived. He kept his shoes on as he walked in and hugged her. His hair was much lighter than Nathalie's, blond as Bijou's. He seemed young; Bijou had told me last week he was twenty-eight. Nathalie was ten or twelve years older than me, but it was enough to make her the adult and me the child. It rattled me, the prospect of being here with someone around the same age as me. I leaned in and whispered to Bijou to remind me of his name. She looked up and told me, then rushed over. "Uncle Ethan!"

Nathalie was motioning for him to take his shoes off, and I saw him hold his hands up as if accosted. I trailed behind Bijou, who stood in the living room, waiting for him to greet her. As Nathalie walked over to Deirdre, he turned to us.

"This is my friend Willa," Bijou said. I blushed as I came up behind her.

"The famous Willa," he said. There was something mocking in how he said it, and I smiled at him uneasily.

"Nice to meet you," I said.

"Where do we put the coats again?" He looked straight at me, and his question hovered between us.

"Oh, in there." I pointed to the cabinet behind his shoulder. He was holding his jacket folded over his arms, and he held it out to me. I looked at it, and without meaning to, my hand shot up to meet his. He laughed.

"Just kidding with you," he said, putting the coat away himself. My face flamed and I went to turn away. "Wait," he said. "Willa what?"

"Chen," I answered.

"No. What Willa are you named after?"

I stared at him. That wasn't what he'd asked at all.

"Like Willa Cather?" he said. "Or 'Willa,' the Stephen King story?"

"Oh," I said. "Cather. My mom liked her in college."

It was something lodged in the depths of my brain. I felt like I'd cursed inside the apartment; I'd never mentioned my mother to them, unprompted. "I'm going to go grab a sweater," I said, and went to sit on my bed for ten seconds, picked up a cardigan even though the heat was on. I knew that Nathalie's mom had lived in this room, and I looked around warily. I felt so stupid for not realizing she wasn't still alive. Had it been that obvious? I'd never questioned why I hadn't seen her in person. I was used to family being something that existed only abstractly.

*

When I walked back out, everyone had rearranged their spots. Bijou brought Ethan a mug, and he strolled to the liquor cart and poured a dash of whiskey in. He left the bottle unscrewed and returned to where Bijou was waiting for him, next to Gabe. Nathalie and Deirdre were in the kitchen, and Tom and Paul were looking out the far window, Paul pointing to things. It felt like being at a party, being at school, where groups were all around me, and I never knew where to join. Where was it safest? I felt too shy to walk up to Bijou when she was around Gabe and Ethan. I could feel Ethan's eyes flick to me, and he leaned into Gabe and said something. Gabe looked straight ahead and frowned as he spoke. I tucked my hair behind my ear and headed for the kitchen, to see if Nathalie needed help. On the way to the kitchen I screwed the cap of the whiskey back on and picked up an empty bowl, crusty with salt from the Marcona almonds everyone had eaten. I left the sweater I'd grabbed on the arm of the couch.

"Should I get more almonds?" I said as I opened the door with my left hand, held the bowl aloft in my right. I pushed the door open with my hip, recognized my own urgency to feel casual, to say, *I live here too.* It mixed with my desire to have a task, to be able to hide behind the excuse of being at work. Deirdre had been hovering close to Nathalie, offering some kind of suggestion, and I could see the wrinkles beside Nathalie's mouth deepening as she set her jaw. I wanted so badly to be useful.

"Are they all gone?" she said. "Do you know where—"

"Got 'em," I said, reaching into the cabinet and pouring more into the bowl. They clattered like little stones. "And the olives?" There was a jar hiding behind the spices, Castelvetrano olives, the only kind Nathalie liked.

"Yes, Ethan loves those. Actually, Deirdre, could you toss those on the table near the boys? Willa, remember how I showed you the other day that kind of dressing Gabe likes?"

Deirdre picked up the bowls, not astute enough to know she was being banned. I inched closer to Nathalie, wondering if she was going to tell me it was all a ruse and she was more comfortable with me.

"The anchovies?" she prompted. "They're in the fridge."

"Oh, right," I said, twirling around. "It's eight of us, so twice the dressing?" She nodded, and I slid out four slimy silver anchovies into a plastic bowl. Nathalie had shown me how to use the tines of a fork to smash them into paste. I chopped two shallots and put them into a mason jar, poured in the vinegar, sprinkled salt and pepper, and added the anchovies. I put the lid back on and presented it to Nathalie. The dressing had to sit for a while before the next step, which I didn't know. She'd only taught me the prep work.

"I'll finish that before we eat." She had a baster in her hand and an apron wedged above her hips, her lips dyed with a hint of red in the center. I thought about the mug I'd seen earlier and looked for it, but she was drinking out of a wineglass, the special-occasion ones.

"Would you like a taste?" she said. "You like wine, right?" I nodded—didn't she remember offering me some before?—and she took down another glass, but a stemless one. "This one's too light for Gabe, so I'm keeping it for myself. Thanks for being here." She poured it into my glass and clinked with me. "Where is . . ." She trailed off for a second, pulled her glass back in front of her lips. "What's your family doing today?" she asked.

She had asked about my family at times, but her attention wasn't focused enough to outlast my skittishness. *My dad lives here, my mom lives here, I don't go home that much.* I changed the subject, and it was easy to prompt her away from prying.

"My mom is at my stepdad's family's house in Long Island, I think," I said. Light pierced through the wine, and my head got a velvety rush. "I don't really go there."

"Lillian is with her husband's family, which is kind of a relief, because her kids are—" She stopped for a second, remembering that she'd already told me this, that she'd brushed off my complaint about her sister's kids just hours ago, and then began speaking even faster. "A lot, as you know, and Jen hasn't come back for Christmas in years, and my dad is on a cruise with his new girlfriend," she said, her voice thick with disdain. "So we're both abandoned." I looked at her curiously as I sipped the wine she'd poured me. Nathalie thought we were both abandoned.

She took a sip. "I can't believe it—two years." I tried to think of how best to say I was sorry, but then she shook her head, remembering herself. "Bijou is excited that you're here." She put the glass of wine down to the left of the stove. "So am I."

I was too embarrassed to say anything back, even as I had one melodramatic thought after the next. *I wouldn't be anywhere else. I'm so glad you invited me. I kind of love you all?* A timer rang, and Nathalie took out the potatoes and couldn't find the pot holders, and I finished my glass of wine, and she sent me back out the door with a platter of cheese. I noticed the hydrangeas, arranged around the room, looking full and upright. I wished that I'd told Nathalie what I'd done, that I'd get credit for the flowers' new life.

*

"Do you know the Stephen King story?" Ethan said as he sat down next to me at the table. Nathalie had called for us to sit down, but I had been the first one to walk over and do so. I shifted in my seat—I'd hoped I might be wedged in between Nathalie and Bijou. I thought about getting up to refill my water from the fridge and sitting back down in another place, but as soon as he spoke, the rest of them descended on the table, pulling out chairs and claiming their spots. Bijou slid into the seat at my right.

"The Stephen King story?" I pulled the napkin from its crystal ring on the plate.

"The one named after you," he said.

"I've never read any Stephen King."

"Willa is a bit of a deep cut. But none? Not even *It*? Or *Carrie*?"

"I've seen the movie of *Carrie*," I lied. I knew enough of the storyline: a lonely girl, a bucket of blood. Revenge. I spread the napkin around my thighs, tucked it underneath at the corners.

The table was set gorgeously. I hadn't known there were wings underneath, that you could pull out half-moons for an elongated feast. The table was reclaimed wood, and Nathalie had draped and bunched up several lace tablecloths and runners, so the wood peeked through the uncovered spots. There was a glass pitcher, already dewy, filled with water and ice and lemons sliced thin as tissue. There were two bottles of red wine already opened on the table, but everyone had a fancy wineglass filled halfway with a chilled white, including me. They didn't normally let me drink with them, or even sit with them at each dinner; sometimes when Gabe and Nathalie were both home, they'd give me a gentle dismissal, saying, "That's about all we need, Willa." I'd know that it was up to me to feed myself, and I'd run out to buy a sandwich, or snack on what was in my mini-fridge.

The sides were scattered around the table: rosemary potatoes in a blue-and-white-patterned china, green beans simmered in tomatoes in a red Le Creuset. The mashed potatoes were heaped like clouds inside a large white bowl. A basket lined with checked napkins was bursting with rolls, and soft circles of butter in clear dishes sat on either side. Nathalie was still in the kitchen, and I saw her bending over, turning the oven light on.

"So, what do you do?" I said to Ethan. I wanted to talk to Deirdre, but she was too far, and I didn't want to be silent.

"He's in school," Bijou said.

"One semester left of my doctorate," he said. "Comparative literature. And I teach. At Princeton. Nathalie went there, too, but I have better grades."

I looked at her; she couldn't hear us.

"Have you graduated?"

I nodded, and he kept looking at me. "I studied psychology," I said. I didn't want to name my non-Ivy League college to him.

"Literature is a kind of psychology." He sounded like he was much older than twenty-eight—like he had a job or a house or a life already. "Do you like to read?"

"I read a lot of poetry." I hadn't told anyone that yet, but it was true, wasn't it?

"I haven't read poetry since undergrad," he said. "Who do you like?"

I'd opened my mouth to answer when Nathalie called my name. "Excuse me," I said, feeling important.

"Can you help me bring these out?" Nathalie gestured to a long oval platter on the counter, holding four pork tenderloins sliced in two-inch pieces. She tore rosemary and sprinkled it on top. "Just about done."

As I set the platter on the empty space in the middle of the table, Nathalie called out, "*Dinner*," in a singsong voice. The guests oohed in chorus, and began serving themselves.

"Let's have a toast," Gabe said. He held his wineglass up, and everyone did the same. "To Deirdre and Paul and Tommy, for making the trip here, and to Ethan for doing the same, and to Nathalie, for making us this lovely meal."

Bijou looked at him intently.

"To Bijou for helping her with the meal, of course, and to Willa, for helping us with Bijou."

Would I ever be able to hear my name normally, not as if I were being picked for something? We clinked glasses, and the pads of my fingers tingled. I had been last. I took a sip. There was a brief lull as everyone picked napkins from rings, forks from settings, and passed potatoes and green beans.

Paul spoke first, asking Gabe how the hospital had been, saying that he heard Gabe had been traveling a lot. Deirdre tried to serve Tom a generous heap of green beans, and he simmered. Bijou leaned over to Nathalie and whispered something in her ear. I felt left out, stuck next to Ethan. I reached out for the nearest side—kale sautéed with navy beans and onions—and ladled a spoonful onto my plate.

"Bijou?" I interrupted. "Do you want some?" *I'm your guest*, I thought irrationally.

"Bijou, sweetie, how is your school year going?" Deirdre asked. I felt relieved to be in the physical middle of a conversation, even if I wasn't included.

"It's going well," Bijou said.

"Bijou loves school," Gabe said. "And she's still studying Mandarin, which she's getting really good at."

"I'm not *good*, Dad, it's my first year."

"But Mandarin is hard, sweetie," Nathalie said. I saw Deirdre glance in my direction at the word *Mandarin*. "It can take more than ten years to become fluent, unless they're immersed," Nathalie said to the table.

"So—Willa," Paul said. "How long have you been with them?"

"Since the end of August," I said.

"Right after what's her name left," Deirdre said to Paul, then turned to me. "And where are you from?"

"New Jersey," I said. But as I expected, they tilted their heads, phrasing the next part of their question with their furrowed brows. I knew what it meant, so I answered. "I'm half Chinese, if that's what you mean."

"Your mom or your dad?" Paul said genially.

"My dad was born in Taiwan."

"In 'Willa,' the story version by Stephen King, does anyone know what the twist is?" Ethan interrupted, twirling his fork into a mound of mashed potatoes. "Willa, our newest guest, you don't know?" I felt my hair sticking to the back of my neck as I shook my head.

"They are in love. It's a love story. A man awakens from his train that has just crashed, and he can't find his fiancée among the wreckage."

At the word *fiancée*, I remembered Nathalie saying that Ethan had one. That was part of why, when they spoke about him, I'd expected him to be much older. Where was she? Ethan tore off a piece of his roll and stuck it into the left side of his mouth as he continued to speak.

"The other passengers tell him the train is about to arrive; he can't go searching for her; it's too dangerous for him. But like Orpheus, he can't help himself. Bijou," he said, turning to her. "Who's Orpheus?"

"Eurydice's husband," she said, as if she were being timed. "He went to the underworld to bring her back to life, but Hades said he couldn't look back at her as they walked out, and he did it anyway."

He reached behind my shoulders to ruffle her hair. His sleeves were rolled up to his elbows, and I noticed his arm was furry with hair so blond it was almost clear.

"Remember when I used to read you all of those, Bee? You don't forget anything." Ethan's voice had the same tone as Nathalie's, melodious with a touch of gravel, but the moment he spoke he seemed so forceful, arrogant, whereas Nathalie had a sort of confident charm.

"So that's right," he said. "A man in love doesn't think clearly! Am I right, Gabriel?" Gabe took off his glasses and polished them. "On his way into town, he's almost mauled by a wolf, but that's not as important in this condensed version. He finds Willa in the corner booth of a bar, all by herself. Music, lights, fogged-up windows."

It was strange to hear him narrate a story about someone else with my name. I'd never met anyone with my name; it sounded so old, like mothballs and lavender. *Willa in the corner booth of a bar, all by herself.* Like a taunt. "He talks about the wreck and the other passengers involved and tries to convince her to come back to the station and get on another train."

"Who would get on another train right after being in a wreck," Deirdre said, and took a neat sip of her wine. Everyone had moved on to red, that first glass having slid down our throats like water. I'd helped myself to the closest bottle, filled my glass up high when no one was watching so I wouldn't have to reach again. Bijou tapped the tines of her fork against her plate, sending little metal vibrations down the table.

"That's kind of it, Dee," he said. "They can't. Because it's revealed that they died in the wreck. That they're ghosts, and all the passengers are ghosts, and only when they realize this can they see a poster tacked up on the station, saying it will be demolished. It's like they're in purgatory, but the only thing keeping them there is their own denial."

He said this last line with emphasis, as if it would underscore the rest of his speech, but it felt like there was a loop missing, and we all waited for it to be tied. I wondered whether Ethan was drunk. Maybe if I was more drunk, this would have been entertaining.

"Yes, life is frail and love is blind, and denial hurts," Nathalie said, as if she'd heard this before. "Does anyone want more tenderloin?"

"Nathalie, this is all delicious," I said, realizing I hadn't complimented her, though I'd already eaten all of mine. Everyone murmured agreement. Gabe took another piece, and so did Tom. Deirdre helped herself to more green beans. I took another scoop of mashed potatoes. I looked from Nathalie to Ethan. They were young to lose their mom. The thought conjured my own, a quick image I had of her a couple Christmases ago, lifting out duck from the oven, a pink bra strap almost at her elbow, her kitchen counter covered with cups and pans. The duck had been overcooked, her first time making it. I'd tried to help her do dishes, but they seemed never-ending. Alex, his eyes like my mom's, showing me his video game collection in the living room. I blinked, rattling the thought back to its cage.

19

Durland, New Jersey, 2005

Even though my mom's front door was often unlocked, I only walked into our house from the back. In the back, there was a small room with a wall of windows that my mom called the sunroom. She kept indoor plants there, birds of paradise and elephant ears next to reading chairs and a child-size table I used to drink pretend tea at with my teddy bears.

I didn't have many memories of my mom and my dad in the same room; I only knew them apart. They divorced when I was too young for me to remember them being together. But of course I saw other families, at school or at their house, at sports games or graduation. Other parents did my mom favors throughout the years: picked me up for school, took me to their house for lunch, took me in for dinner, drove me to the mall. The other mothers were so much calmer, more assured, their hair in blonde helmets around their heads and their chins tilted down at me. The fathers were there. They weren't asked to do much. But still, I saw them. The way they came in and kissed the tops of heads, the way they loosened ties and pushed up sleeves before sinking to the floor to scoop something up, how they reached bowls from the top cabinets and brought things from one room to the next. There was so little asked of them; it was hard to understand how one couldn't fill that role.

I tried to remember them together. I thought hard—could I see them lying in bed together, making me breakfast, his arm around her shoulder? All I remembered was the first Halloween after he left. He came to visit me after I had gone trick-or-treating. I was wearing a ghost costume, something white that tied around my neck and swung around my wrists. He sat in my mom's reading chair in the sunroom and looked so uncomfortable, so out of place. Like he was a visitor. Like he had never seen this room before, like he had lived his whole life somewhere else.

The elephant ears were drooping, deadened stems dragging their leaves on the floor. My mom's reading chair was now her breastfeeding chair, and next to it was an errant pacifier and a stained blue bib, the cushion she used to prop Alex on when she opened her robe to feed him. The chair was turned away to face the windows, and hanging over the back of it was a stained dish towel. *Gross*, I said to myself as I walked to the stairs. I didn't turn the lights on, so I didn't see another bib, a small white one, on the first step, and when I stepped on it, I slipped. I caught myself on the banister but not before slamming my shin on the first step. I sank to the floor, holding my calf between my hands. The pain was so bright and blinding that my eyes prickled with tears. *Ouch*, I thought, sounding the word out inside my head. I was so good at being quiet, I told myself as I pressed my lips together. Then I heard the door at the top of the stairs open, and I pulled myself up.

When I first met Ray, I didn't hate him. I didn't know I could. I remembered how he would watch *Cops* in the living room and let me stay to see them snapping arms behind backs, cursing and cuffing and kicking. It felt wrong to watch violence like that, unrestrained and unpunished, and I would back out of the room, uneasy, as he clapped his hands together like it was football.

"*Hey*," he said as he started down the stairs.

"Hello," I said as I walked up, as if he'd been greeting me.

"What time is it? *Hey*," he said again. We were in the middle of the stairs, and he grabbed a fistful of my sleeve to jerk me into place. "Do you know what time it is?"

"Not really." It was useless to respond to him; he talked as if he couldn't hear me.

"And you wake us up? You wake Alex up?"

"No one woke up." My voice came out steady even though I could feel my heartbeat in my throat, in my wrists, in my throbbing shin. Alex was asleep; I'd hear him crying if he wasn't, like I heard him crying all the time.

"Don't you see me standing here?"

I stared into his eyes, crawling with red veins. They were a light brown not unlike my own. His breath was stale, like he hadn't brushed his teeth. I cocked my head, playing unaffected. I didn't know where that came from, but I knew I couldn't let him see that I felt anything. I thought of my mom, a light sleeper, how she must have been propped up on her elbow after she felt him arise, how she must have been listening to every word.

"What is the matter?" I said loudly. It wasn't an appropriate response, but I wanted her to hear my voice, how it didn't waver.

"Be quiet," Ray said. "My family is sleeping." He went back to the room and shut the door behind him with a thud.

My chest deflated, my pulse still skipping. Same as always. Sometimes I wished Ray were as tough or as interesting as he thought he was; maybe then he'd do something drastic enough that I'd get to leave. He was a normal guy with a slight anger problem, someone who would scream or throw things, but never use his hands. I guessed that was why my mom thought it was okay. Her father, my grandfather—he used his hands. He was the kind of person who could win an argument, a history professor with an encyclopedic memory and a drinking problem. Every day he'd drink five whiskeys and quiz her on Civil War generals at the dinner table. If she didn't get it right, she'd have a bruise on her upper arm, above her knee, the soft space of her stomach—wherever her clothes would cover. In some ways, Ray was nothing like him. A security guard who only drank beer, who could make two soggy arguments but was easily defeated. It was as if she thought the intellect was the part she should run from.

I heard their mattress groan once as Ray got back into bed, and I went back downstairs. I hadn't eaten dinner. I was used to walking around the house and noticing the full sink of plates and pans, the cobwebs that spread out from corners, the leftover food hardening on plates, but they only made me want to criticize my mom, not keep her afloat. I looked at them and relieved myself of responsibility. They were the remnants of her new family, to which I didn't belong. If someone asked me, which no one did, I'd tell them how my mom never made dinner for me. But she did, sometimes. How else would a pot of spaghetti with Ragú appear on the stove a few times a week? Sometimes it was bell peppers stuffed with ground turkey, or potato leek soup.

Offerings prepared and left on the stove, to be eaten alone. She'd already begun to detach herself from the other parts of motherhood I wanted her for—scratching my back while I fell asleep, picking me up from school, filling out my permission forms or attending back-to-school night. And so I resented this measly gift of sustenance, to be shared with the invaders of our home. I wished that the pots never appeared. I wished she would just let me starve, and be done with it.

20

Kent, New York, 2005

We called my grandma Nai Nai because she was my dad's mother. There was a different word for it if it was your mom's mother. But since my mom wasn't Chinese, I had no idea what it was. That summer I stayed with my dad, Nai Nai also came to stay for a week. They set up a bed in their downstairs den for her so she didn't have to climb the stairs, and she'd cook us tea eggs and pork belly and fried rice, and watch movies in the living room. I wanted to ask her things, but I didn't know how.

I'd always known that my grandfather had died when my dad was twenty-six, right after I was born. That seemed adult, ten years older than I was, but I guessed it was also kind of young. Maybe it made my dad sad that his father never met his daughters, or his current wife. I wondered if he missed his father, as I missed my own. Ten more years wouldn't be enough time.

Though my dad didn't talk much about his childhood, the mythology of it felt as memorized as if it were a comic book I'd paged through daily as a kid. Sometimes I wasn't sure how I had heard these stories, or why they felt like precious stones, but I found myself clinging to them, the few things I knew. How he'd moved here when he was ten without a word of English, and showed up at public school; watched American sitcoms to study; been held against a locker as his eyes were pulled at. How he'd gotten suspended for pushing a kid into a trash can, after being called a chink. Once I found that word shoved into the slats of my locker, scrawled on a flyer for the talent show. I held it between my hands and became aware of the blood swimming between my ears. I thought about bringing it home, but my dad wouldn't be coming to get me for eleven days. If I showed it to my mom, I'd have to explain it to her, this hot, airless feeling. I folded it neatly into thirds, tucked it between my books, and threw it out in an empty bathroom.

One day Nai Nai was in the kitchen. She had a pot of boiling water on the stove and ingredients for fried rice laid out on the counter. Hers was different from the kind at restaurants, hard kernels of rice tinged brown, falling out of the carton like pebbles. It was simple and colorful, white rice dotted with green peas, yellow strips of egg, and chopped-up shrimp and ham. She seemed annoyed that we liked it so much, said that fried rice was for leftovers, but she made it for us anyway.

I shyly stood by the doorway. "Could I help?" I asked.

She pulled out a long rectangle of pork belly from the boiling pot, and ran it under cold water from the sink. "While this cools, you can chop the shrimp. Your dad bought them too big."

I stood next to her and reached for the watery bag of gray shrimp. She normally used the frozen pre-cooked mini shrimp, no bigger than a pinky, and my dad had bought these fresh, each curl larger than my index finger. The knife dragged as I cut them into thirds. It felt strange in my grip; we never cooked at my mom's or chopped things together, and I hoped I was doing it right. I wanted to ask what my dad was like as a child. I wanted to ask what she was like as a child. My tongue lay still in my mouth. "Do you have any siblings?" I finally said.

"You've met my sister. She came to New York that time, on my birthday, ten years ago."

"Oh, yeah," I said. There was a glimpse of a memory—a lazy Susan at a big glass table, a tiny cup of tea, watching the plates spin round and round. "I don't remember talking to her, though."

"You couldn't! She doesn't speak much English, and you kids, none of you can speak Mandarin or Shanghainese, can you."

"Oh. Which one do you speak to your sister?"

"We speak in Shanghainese," she said.

"What's different about Shanghainese?"

She was chopping up a flat yellow omelet into thin strips. "It's softer. Melodic."

"Can Dad speak it?"

"No, no. Your father learned Mandarin. We were in Taiwan. But now—" She blew out air. "Now he can't speak anything at all." She tipped her cutting board full of peppers and omelets into a silver wok on the stove, already full of rice. "It's important the rice be a day old," she said. "Even two days is fine. You don't want it fresh." She swirled the rice around in the oil and then cleared out a little well in the center where you could see the wok. She tipped in more oil and cracked an egg into the empty space. I watched her hands as she worked; they were wrinkled, but they looked soft, moisturized, almost iridescent in their sheen. Long, thin fingers and curved, clean nails. She stirred the yellow yolk into the rice, and it absorbed, then vanished. I'd heard her say how she hated cooking for her husband's whole family when they first got married, but if she hated cooking for her son's, she didn't mention it. Maybe there would be a time when it felt easier to ask her things, after I spent more time with her and wasn't so stilted. She motioned at me to tip in the shrimp. I did and watched as they blushed pink. The wok sizzled, steam lifted up, and for a few seconds I felt obscured by it.

"What was Dad like as a kid?" I said in a rush.

I didn't think she had heard me at first. The steam dissipated, and I could see her face again. Her eyebrows, for as long as I'd known her, had been drawn on, and her hair was still black, with wiry gray weaving through. Sometimes, people said I looked like her when she was young. I wondered if I would look like her when I was old. I wondered how different I would be if my mom had been the Chinese one, instead of my dad. If she'd made me congee with pork floss in the morning rather than pancakes, spoke to me in two languages rather than one. Or how different I'd be if I'd grown up tucked under my dad's arm rather than holding on to my mom's. I watched myself fray in three directions, and didn't know where I wanted to be.

"When I was working, I'd come home and the kids would be with their nanny. I'd come home, and they'd be getting a treat, like a cookie, from her. She had these cookies she'd bring once a week from her town, and she'd bring one for each of the kids. And I'd say, 'Oh, can I have a bite?' I was joking, to see what they'd do. 'Can I have some?' And his sisters would look at their cookies, like, thinking of how much to break off to give to me, and your dad would—he'd walk right over and give me his whole cookie. He'd never even have a bite." I looked at her, this story piercing the space behind my eyes. "Too generous," she said, "from the start."

*

The summer passed uneventfully. I was the same person. But one day my dad did put breakfast in front of me, different from before. A scorched piece of bread with two pats of butter melting. Four strips of bacon making thick curls, tiny bubbles of grease foaming white. Two eggs, crispy at the edges and wobbling in the center, staring up at me like twin suns I could open to the world. The yolk so bright it was almost orange, organic eggs cracked open to show insides like Sunny D. I looked at my plate. It could have been a diner breakfast anywhere in America, so much food it teetered over the edge. *Ordinary*, I told myself, but it felt seismic. My dad didn't look at me after handing it off. But it felt like a language I knew. I bit the bacon in half, pressing the waves of fat against the roof of my mouth. I chomped the hard parts between molars. I cut and mixed eggs until their colors were combined and ate each bite, from soft middle to burnt lacy edge. I soaked bread in yolk, used it as an extension of my tongue, making it lick the plate for me as I finished the entire thing.

"You say you wished you lived with him," my mom had said before I left. She was cradling Alex in her left arm while his mouth was suctioned to her breast. Her breasts had gotten giant and veiny, and I saw them all the time, so white they were almost blue and her nipples almost purplish red where before they'd been pastel, how each of them filled up his whole infant mouth. He was suckling away as she swayed her hips, a towel over her other shoulder, her hair matted and curling out of its ponytail. "You act like I'm such a terrible mom," she said.

"You are," I said back. And even though she had been the one to say it first, I'd seen how her eyes, the blue ones I wished I'd inherited, the eyes that Alex had gotten, filled with tears, and she blinked them away. "You're a terrible mom," I repeated.

"Lucky you," she'd replied. "Have a great summer with your perfect dad."

When I came back at the end, I could have told her the truth, how many days I'd spent lonely and bored, how many nights I'd wanted to call her. But when I returned, I told her only about that morning, the eggs my dad had made me, how he had known exactly what I wanted.

21
New York City, 2014

In January, there was a long break in activities. Normally, Bijou said, they might go skiing for a couple of weeks, or fly to Mexico or Hawaii. "But," she confided in me after they returned from Gabe's parents' after the New Year, "Daddy can't take any more time off work." That meant that there were three weeks left without school, Mondays with no dance, Tuesdays with no violin. Thursdays would have been Mandarin, if Nathalie hadn't canceled it.

"Vacation!" I said to Bijou on the first Monday without school. "We can lie around all day and watch movies." We'd spent months together, but so much of our time was spent on the move. I was a nanny, but what that really meant was that I was her shepherd—taking her from one place to another, constantly, so that lots of our conversations hinged upon logistics. We were going to be late to dance, we had to get home for dinner, violin practice ended early and why wasn't I waiting, we had one hour left before bedtime, should we take the subway or walk? Winter break loomed ahead of me eerily; I would actually have to keep her entertained. I wouldn't be able to duck into a movie at eleven in the morning the way I often did while Bijou was in school, losing myself happily in an empty theater with my feet propped up on the seat in front of me. I wanted help watching her from their giant TV, their soft couch—we could maroon ourselves for hours, drinking hot chocolate and staring at the screen.

"Willa," Nathalie's voice floated in. I jumped. I hadn't known she was in her office. "Can you take Bijou out to do something? Ice-skating, a museum? I don't want her cooped up inside all day."

It was twenty degrees out, but we went. Rather than go to Rockefeller Center, I took her to a trendy hotel on the West Side that had an ice rink set up in front. I held on to the railing, and Bijou skated backward past me. "Can you take a photo of me?" she asked. I maneuvered my body so my back was against the rail and took out my cell phone. Where had she learned to do this? We took the subway to the Cloisters, and it was faster than I thought, forty minutes on the express train and we spilled out in Washington Heights. Snow hung heavy on the branches and huge swaths of it were unbroken, still sparkly from the night before. I was wearing two pairs of leggings underneath my jeans, and my fingers felt numb from the cold even under my gloves, but I hadn't been prepared for how beautiful it could look, even so. In the gift shop, we warmed up, blowing on our hands. "Want a magnet?" I asked. The next day we went uptown to the Museum of Natural History, walking in circles around the giant whale, staring at the wildlife. After that I was out of things to do and thought that if I came up with an indoor activity, maybe we wouldn't be forced out into the cold. After breakfast, I brought a pile of catalogs into Bijou's bedroom and proposed making collages, loudly, so that Nathalie would hear. Bijou brought out construction paper and scissors that cut zig-zags and scalloped circles, glue sticks and glitter that tapped out. I looked at the photos sitting on her desk.

"Your grandma, right?" I said. I'd been wondering how to bring her up ever since Bijou had told me—reminded me?—that she wasn't with us. Nathalie must have told me before; I must not have been listening. Sometimes I did this when I was self-conscious, thought endlessly about what I was doing wrong and ignored the person I was worried about pleasing. "What do you miss about her?"

"A lot," she said.

We cut into magazines quietly, the only sound the tearing of glossy paper, the smooth glide of the scissors. "My grandfather died when I was a baby," I said.

"I'm sorry," she said automatically.

"No, it's just—I mean, I don't remember him." I watched as she opened a desk drawer and took out a ruler, holding it against a magazine page as she cut. "What did you call her?"

"Nana," she said. "I've told you that."

This is like pulling teeth, I thought. Then I looked at her and said it. "This is like pulling teeth." I poked her in the side, trying to make her laugh. "I'm just asking!"

"Okay, okay. Well. She'd come over and do nothing, because she never worked. She lived here for a while but then after she moved back to her house she would come in to see me every week." Bijou said. "We would plan my restaurant together."

"Your restaurant? Oh, the one you'll have when you grow up?"

She nodded. "She'd always take me out to dinner and she'd say it was research. For mine. Mom usually goes to cycling on Monday nights. We'd go to fancy places. Mom would get mad at her for taking me to such fancy places."

"Like where?" My voice was tentative; I didn't want her to clam up again.

"Once we had a pasta tasting menu at Babbo." She giggled. "She and Mom kind of had a fight about it."

"Doesn't your mom take you out to dinner?" I asked.

"Not just me and her. With Nana it was like . . . a secret thing. The two of us. No one else."

I looked down at her lap and saw she'd been cutting out according to a color scheme, her lap littered with blues and greens. A triangle of a wave, an oval of grass, a cerulean tear.

"I know what you mean," I said. I turned the page to an advertisement for a horror show, and cut around a dangling key.

22

New York City, 2014

February: long, gray days, back to school and schedules, back to walks to dance and walks home from violin, back to holding her violin case in a gloved hand, burning my lip on tea as I hurried to school, to the sun leaking out of the sky before dinner was over. To sunsets we watched from the living room, with the heat up and hot chocolate mix on the stove.

Whenever Donna washed my clothes, I came home to cotton thongs folded in thirds in the top drawer, my jeans ironed and put away, my jackets zipped to the collar and back on the hanger. She washed everyone else's clothes three times a week. They had a set of machines hidden in a closet, and at first, I did my own laundry. But once I was accidentally doing it at the same time she was, and she noticed how little I had, and it turned into her coming into my room on Fridays and throwing mine in as well.

The first time I noticed something that wasn't mine, it was a light pink camisole, a soft stretchy fabric with a sheen when crinkled under the light. I thought about running right to Nathalie, handing it to her still in its fold. But then I pulled off my shirt and unhooked my bra. I shimmied it over my torso. My nipples poked through the thin fabric. It had looked too small for me hanging between my fingers, but once on it felt like a second skin. I was going to give it back to her, but it was so soft. I pulled my T-shirt on over it and wore it for the rest of the day. By the end of the day it smelled like me, so I couldn't give it back. I wore it the whole week, tossing it in my hamper at the end, not sure where it would end up after it was washed. It didn't happen that often. If it was something obvious, like a pair of jeans, I'd leave it at the mouth to her closet, and she'd pick it up. We never spoke about these mistakes. I wasn't even sure if she knew where my drop-offs were coming from. Her closet was a full-sized room. Maybe she never noticed anything was missing at all.

*

"*Caaaarrie.*" His voice was singsong, playful. I'd gone shopping that day because I knew no one would be home when I came back with the bags. I got in the elevator with three bags, a week's worth of salary, and when it opened, there was Ethan.

I was startled and let out a yelp when I saw him. "Why are you calling me that? Isn't Stephen King a little lowbrow for a literature professor?" I caught my breath.

"You're right. I don't even really care for him. I guess I have a tendency to hold on to jokes," he said. He stood there coolly, hands in the pockets of his khaki-colored jeans. "I actually love the name Willa. It reminds me of my favorite tree."

I steadied myself against the wall as I pushed off my shoes. He was standing so close to me.

"A weeping willow," he said.

"What are you doing here? I thought you went back to school?"

"I'm finding the library a bit . . . creatively stifling for my dissertation. Needed a change of scenery," he said. "I'm gonna stay in Nat's office for a while, the couch is a pullout. Since someone's in the guest room. Lillian's dinner this week and all. Do you like weeping willows? We had one in our backyard growing up. We used to sit under it and read."

"I don't know that I've ever seen one," I said. "Excuse me." He followed me as I began to walk toward my room, and I halted. "Lillian's dinner?"

"There's one in Morningside Park," he said. "It's Lillian's birthday tomorrow. She's coming in for dinner. Wonder if you'll be joining us? Gabe's excused, visiting his mom—I'm sure you knew that."

"I'll be back out in a minute. If you'll stay here."

He laughed a little, held his palms up the same way he'd done to Nathalie, and backed away. In my room, I put the tissue paper bundles on the bed and folded up the shopping bags. I put them in the closet on the floor with the others. I didn't know what to spend my money on without rent, and a faint tug in my head told me the answer wasn't a leather skirt and a cashmere-blend scarf. But that reasoning felt far away when I lived among high-thread-count sheets and handwoven mohair blankets.

I thought I heard the elevator and that Nathalie had come home. But when I walked back out, Ethan was gone.

I'd thought he wanted to talk to me.

*

Nathalie was in fact having Lillian over for dinner, and after an awkward pause, she did ask me to join. Lillian looked like Nathalie but rounder, less angular; cheekbones not as sharp, hair that fell in curls. She wore jeans and colorful sweaters with collars poking out, with sparkling bracelets on her wrist and too much blush. *I would not want to work for this woman*, I thought. And at dinner, the two of them got drunk. Her kids were not there, just her, and us, and Bijou, who was scooping up green beans as if they were gummy bears. Every so often she refilled her mound from the glass bowl in front of her and dug back in. I looked around the table, still starving. I had taken one of the smaller pieces of arctic char, not wanting to be greedy, but now leftover pink fillets lay half-eaten on everyone else's plates. There was nothing within reach to take. The platter with the fish was on the other side of the table; the beefsteak tomatoes with sliced mozzarella were across two candlesticks. On my side, we had the green beans and the broccoli. Next to me, Ethan reached his arm across the table and grabbed for a roll, tucked within a wooden basket with a white cloth napkin like at a restaurant. I imagined them still warm and saw him smear a thick pat of butter inside. My arms weren't long enough to reach. It was better to starve than to ask Ethan for help. I jabbed at the last stalk of broccoli on my plate.

Nathalie and her siblings, Bijou, and I. I shouldn't have been there, but I was. They were all going to go out for martinis after I put Bijou to bed, they told me, but staring at the empty bottles of wine littering the table, I wasn't sure they'd make it. Nathalie held a palm to her cheek. The light from the overhead chandelier spun off the sweat-sheen that peeked from their hairlines and flushed cheeks. Ethan seemed to notice this at the same time I did and reached across the table again to take the bottle of wine from in front of Nathalie.

"You're both all red," he said pointedly.

Nathalie ignored him. "Bee, do you want dessert?"

Ethan and Bijou had the same shiny blond hair, like champagne in a clear glass. Bijou chewed and then swallowed three oily green beans, her mouth shiny at the corners. "In a little, Mom."

"I made flourless chocolate cakes," Nathalie said. "You love those."

Bijou picked the serving spoon back up. Its handle looked like a tree branch dropped into a vat of silver paint, and poked the soft points of your hands when you gripped it. Bijou wrapped her fingers around it anyway, but in her small grip, it looked overgrown. Stray green beans dropped onto the carpet, two landing neatly on her skirt.

"Oh, no," Bijou said without moving, looking at me. I picked them off and put them back on her plate, the greasy residue like two parallel matchsticks.

"Let's put some water on it," I said. The kitchen was a few steps away, behind the french doors, and we both pushed back our chairs and went inside.

"But it's oil. Water isn't going to help," she said in a stage whisper, like she hadn't wanted to embarrass me at the table. I squirted three drops of dish soap on top of a wet paper towel, showing her the method Nathalie had told me. She stood still as I rubbed it in circles over the stain, then nodded to the oven, where the cakes were staying warm. We prepared two trays laden with five separate cakes and little forks, with a pint container of vanilla ice cream on each tray. I was so used to this now, the trays, utensils, endless bowls for serving, that I'd probably do it forever, if I ever moved out.

"Dessert," I said when we came back out, my voice drifting off. They were talking loudly about something.

"Please help yourselves, everyone," Nathalie said, gesturing to the platters. I didn't really want cake, but I was still so hungry, so I took one to my seat and sat back down. I thought about what I had stored in my kitchenette—a couple of yogurts, some dried mango. I dug my spoon into the center of the cake.

"Do you have tea?" Lillian said.

Nathalie nodded. "Of course."

"Willa—green? A Japanese kind, preferably? I'm sure you know best."

My muscles wrapped around each other again. I was tired of this constant edge. Nathalie and Gabe weren't perfect, but any prejudices of theirs were neatly tucked away, in a place I didn't have to see; Ethan, Lillian, they were different. And yet everything ended with me feeling like the discomfort was my fault. If I made too big a deal about it, if I acted upset. And even if I didn't, like when her kids had held up their eyes, a cloud still lingered over everything, leaving me to dispel the gloom. So I stood up and started to make tea, filling the kettle with water, standing by and waiting for it to boil. I'd carried my half-eaten cake in to finish, but my stomach had turned stormy, so I scraped off the plate and put it in the dishwasher. I wasn't sure why I was so angry; I made tea for Nathalie and Bijou all the time. It was part of what I was paid for. It was part of why I'd been included in this dinner, sitting at their table. I heard the three of them debating about a memory from their youth, the time Ethan had been chauffeured home in a cop car from a party.

"It is past *your* bedtime, Miss Bee," Nathalie said. "You're going to get the wrong ideas if you hear too much more of your uncle's bad behavior. Willa? Bedtime?"

In two trips I brought out three mugs of water, and several little boxes of tea, the green kind from Starbucks among them. "Let's go, Bee," I said. Her spoon clattered in her bowl. Lillian sat up and reached for the boxes, riffling through. "A spoon?" she asked, wincing at her own request. I went back to the kitchen and pulled out three spoons, folding them into each other on the table.

"Okay, good night, my sweet niece," Lillian said. "Come give me a big hug. I'll see you soon, okay?" She made three loud wet smacks on Bijou's cheek.

"Bee, meet me in your bedroom, okay?" I went to pour myself a mug of tea. I liked having chamomile at night. Tomorrow, Lillian would be gone. I wouldn't need to deal with her again. I closed the kitchen doors behind me and shut off the lights.

"Good night, everyone," I said awkwardly, and turned away.

"Oh, gosh, this tea is hot," Lillian said.

"It's tea," Nathalie said, in a girlish giggle.

"Omigod, I know. But I can't drink it this way. Could someone bring me a few cubes of ice?" Lillian said, prompting an expansive, open silence from the room, as everyone waited for someone else to do it. Maybe they were waiting for me. I had turned from the table, already shut the doors. *The kitchen is closed*, I thought. I had to do my real job—putting Bijou in bed. But no one else had moved. I found myself unable to keep walking away. Were they waiting for me? I thought about sticking my hand right into Ethan's water glass, plunging my fingers into his lemon-tinged water and coming up with a fistful of melted ice. I thought about dropping the cubes into Lillian's glass, one by one, or all at once, in a tumbling splash. It was the only rebellion I could dream up. But wouldn't that still be doing what she asked?

23
New York City, 2014

When a college friend canceled on dinner with me, I didn't want to tell Nathalie. I went out so little, so I thought I'd head out and pretend I was going to dinner anyway. As she began the routine of dismissing me—checking if there were dishes in the sink I could wash, and making sure Bijou didn't need anything she didn't want to do herself—she cursed softly to herself.

"You said you're going out tonight, right?"

"I don't have to," I said casually.

"No, I was—ah, never mind." She glanced at her watch and then to the window.

"What is it?"

"I was wondering what neighborhood you were going to. I left my credit card at Monique last night. Do you know it, on Hudson? I meant to stop by earlier, and it's actually the one I need for tomorrow morning. I could run over and get it, but if it's close to where you're going . . ."

"That *is* close to where I'm going, actually," I said.

I got dressed in everything I'd bought the week before: a stiff leather skirt that pushed out in a triangle from my hips, a silky black button-down shirt, and my new scarf looped around my neck. Monique was warm and shadowy, copper light falling around the oval bar in the center of the room. Normally I felt too self-conscious to go to a bar by myself, but I had a reason to be there—Nathalie had asked me to be. I pulled myself into a stool with no one around it. A brunette bartender in a tank top gave me a glass of water and a cocktail list. I wanted wine, but still didn't know what kind I liked or how to ask the bartender to choose. I'd worked at a bar once, but we mostly served beer-and-shot deals, ice-filled vodka sodas. Our two house wines came in giant screw-top jugs. I worked there ten months and never had to open a bottle. I scanned the list and found one that someone had ordered for me once.

"Can I have a glass of the falanghina?" *Fah-lin-ghee-na.* I liked the way my mouth curled around the word; the long *e* felt glamorous. She poured a thin-stemmed glass to the halfway point and winked at me in a casual, friendly way I'd never be able to imitate. The pale wine rushed like salt onto my tongue.

"Do you want to start a tab?" she asked.

"Actually, my boss left her card here last night, and I'm supposed to pick it up for her. Nathalie Adrien. She should have called before." Here in this bar full of men in suits and women in sheath dresses, the word *boss* meant I could be her assistant at an art gallery, an architecture firm, a publishing house. No one knew that I'd had to massage lice shampoo into her daughter's hair last week. The bartender went to check for the card, and I sipped at my wine. I'd add it to Nathalie's tab.

I saw a woman sitting across the bar from me by herself with a glass of red wine. She had such good posture; I lifted my shoulders up, looking at her. *Someone else by herself,* I thought happily. But then a man in a suit rushed in and put his hands on her shoulders, kissing one of her cheeks. It was just after 8:00 PM, and I looked around—this seemed like a bit of a date bar, not a work place. I wasn't the only person here by myself; there were a few others. But I noticed that there were lots of tables of two, fingers touching near candlelight. I continued sipping my salty wine and looked around like I was watching television. Maybe I'd even have another drink. Nathalie didn't think I would be home for hours.

"Waiting for someone?" a voice said behind my right ear. I turned. He was leaning on the back of the stool next to me, his credit card out, no drink in his hand.

"Just coming from work," I said. "Having a drink before I go home." Was that what a regular working person would say? I realized I hadn't answered his question.

"I'm in the same boat." He edged the stool out slightly but didn't sit. "Do you live nearby?"

"In Tribeca," I said. "You?"

"I'm a few blocks from here," he said, nodding out onto the West Village street. I watched his impression form of who I was based on my neighborhood, and I formed mine of him. "May I sit?" he asked.

I nodded. He asked what I was drinking. The bartender still hadn't addressed him, and I felt special. I answered him, like it was something I ordered each night after leaving my office.

"Do you want another?" he asked. My glass had only a half-moon of wine left, and I nodded. The bartender came back at that moment with Nathalie's card. I'd seen her get delayed making a round of cocktails for a table of six by the window.

"Here's your card, hon. Another glass?"

"You can add it to mine," he said, and handed her his card. "I'll have an old-fashioned."

"Thank you," I said. Sometimes letting someone buy me a drink made me nervous, the debt they held from it. But holding Nathalie's card between my hands made me feel safe. I could always change my mind.

"My pleasure. I'm Andrew. Andrew Hunter." I didn't understand why people gave their full names upon meeting each other. He looked down at the card between my hands. "And you're Nathalie?"

I followed his gaze to the card, her name peeking out from between my fingers like I was brandishing it. I tilted my head to the side in a way that might be construed as a nod. I couldn't bring myself to fully say no.

"It's nice to meet you," he said. "What do you do?"

My face warmed; I didn't know why I'd done that. He'd made it too easy. I thought about giving him her job, but he looked like he might be in finance too—he was a white man wearing a nice suit. "I'm an executive assistant—I mean, well, like a personal assistant."

"I think that's what all executive assistants end up being," he said, like it was funny, so I smiled to appease him.

"What about you?" I said.

He named something and told me it was a hedge fund. Personal assistant was barely a lie, I thought proudly. I *was* like a personal assistant.

"What industry?" he asked.

A few options whirred through my head, but which would he be furthest away from? "Fashion," I said.

"What kinds of things do you assist on?" he said.

"Oh, everything," I said. "I manage her appointments, her schedule, you know. She travels a lot. I also have to pick up her dry cleaning, things like that, get her kid from school."

"Her kid?" he said. "No boundaries, huh?"

"Well, we're close," I said. "I mean, she has a nanny, it was just a time or two."

"I won't tell," he said. "I've heard that bosses in fashion can be brutal."

"No, she's great. We're close," I repeated. "She tells me I can take days off, you know, a vacation, if I need. And she gives me things, like presents, like, I mean, things she doesn't want. She's really smart," I said, faltering. I hadn't spoken to a stranger in so long. It was like I had forgotten the arc of small talk, its predictable turns.

"Have you taken any vacations lately?" he said.

I shook my head. "No. Have you?"

"Oh, no. My boss—*not* keen on the vacation day. But sometimes he does give me things he doesn't want."

I blushed—how stupid I'd sounded. "What kind of things are those?" I took the last sip of my wine as the bartender came over with our next round.

"Cheers," he said seriously. "Oh, you know. Mandatory work on the weekends. Clients he hates that I have to take out for drinks. Breakfast meetings. Tickets to musicals, *never* the Jets games."

I watched him talk and felt a watery sort of appreciation for how normal he was. White, tall, brown hair, a button-down shirt with a checked pattern that fit well, and his shoes looked expensive. He wasn't that good-looking, but he was good-looking enough. Average across the board. That was a type too. Nathalie had Gabe. Lots of young artists had boring boyfriends paying their rent. But it wasn't like I was an artist, had any sort of aura to outshine his. His stubble was two or three days old, probably on its last day before he had to shave it for work.

"What do you get that you don't want?" he asked.

I thought about it. I liked this game. "So much!" I said, rushing to get it out. "Gluten-free artisanal bread—I'm not gluten-free. Or like, old clothes that don't fit me that she doesn't want to sell. Jars of moisturizer that are half-full. I pretended once that I liked chardonnay, and so now I have to act like I like chardonnay, but I hate it. Lice!" I said suddenly, and he made a small but perceptible movement backward. "Lice—her kid's class had lice and—" I remembered with a drop in my stomach that I had to lie. "I had to go buy the shampoo for her nanny to put on. Since she wouldn't do it herself."

He let out a breath. "No lice situations with my boss, thankfully. Though when I was younger, I did have a boss who made me bring Pedialyte and eggs to his house whenever he was hungover in the morning. And his place was disgusting. I was always relieved I wasn't his housekeeper. I always told myself, it could be worse. I guess in your case, at least you're not her nanny?"

I saw the tea light candles on the bar, wavering in the air. I saw the bartender circling the room, collecting orders and empty glasses. I saw last sips being funneled into mouths, first sips taken delicately, middle sips like gulps. It was one of those moments where I felt like people might be looking at me.

How could he have known? He didn't, I reminded myself. And I laughed, like it was funny. "It could be worse," I agreed.

"That was when I was an assistant too," he said. "It's all hazing. Someone has to do the bad shit. And then in a few years, you get to do it to someone else."

I looked at him, how certain he seemed. "But why would you want to? Couldn't you just stop it? The hazing?"

He took a sip and pressed his lips together, as if he didn't know how to break something to me. "I mean, someone has to buy coffee. Or—lice shampoo." He smiled and nudged my elbow with his. "I'm sure you'll have an assistant to send out for lice shampoo in no time."

"But what if you're the nanny?" He looked at me blankly. "Like—you're telling me I can look forward to hazing my assistant once I finish being an assistant. But what's the progression if you're the nanny in this situation?"

"Well. That's like—another world. The nanny's not going to have an assistant, like . . ." He waved his arm up, thinking, then brushed his hand through his hair. "The janitor doesn't turn into CEO. I mean, he doesn't want to. He can't."

"I don't know that you can say either of those things," I said. I didn't know what I was trying to say, but I knew that I wanted to say something. "That he doesn't want to. That he can't." My voice sounded sullen, quieter than I'd have liked, but still, it was there.

"You know what? You're right," he said, and I couldn't tell if it was gentle or condescending. He held up his hand to gesture for two more drinks. I looked at the air his finger had wagged in; I hadn't said I wanted another one.

"What do you do to your assistant?" I asked.

He leaned in closer. "My assistant *loves* me. I'd even let you call her to check."

"I think calling your assistant at 9:00 PM to tell a girl at a bar you're a good boss kind of proves the opposite," I said, but I laughed halfway through, and so did he.

"Okay, okay. Well, if you think of another way for me to prove it to you, let me know."

As I looked at him, my chest lit up with the simple rush of someone bending to my will. I was the bender in my life. I did what Bijou wanted, what Nathalie wanted, and from their satisfaction I derived a sort of pleasure from a job well done. I did, truly, feel pleased when they were happy, a contented busyness that allowed me to relax. So close to happiness, I could see someone else tasting it, and imagine it melting onto my tongue.

His old-fashioned arrived in a new glass, and the bartender descended with a brand-new bottle she opened in front of me and poured from. I saw the inevitable question of the end of the evening hang in the air. I thought about what it would feel like to give in to it. This was the longest I'd ever gone without having sex, and I counted the months in my head as they ticked forward—six, seven, now eight. I felt monastic, like it was all part of a plan. But in front of the first guy who had shown interest in me in months, I was torn by my automatic excitement, the way that other face clicked on. How as we continued to talk, I found myself tilting my chin at him, perching forward on my stool.

The ice in his old-fashioned clinked as he took his second-to-last sip. "You're funny," he said. "So, would you . . . want to continue this elsewhere? I do live just a few blocks away."

"I'm not sure," I said.

"Sure, I understand," he said. "Maybe I could get your number? We could have dinner sometime."

What would Nathalie have said, if she didn't want to have dinner with him, if she did want to cut to the other part? What was she doing here the night she left her card? I'd noticed it was her personal one, not her corporate. "How many blocks?" I said. I watched his Adam's apple as he signed the check, the push of it to his throat, and it felt strange to think, *Soon I can touch that if I want.* I thought of the cost of my wine, seventeen dollars a glass, and wondered if I should have gotten one more, as if it'd be like pocketing a crumpled twenty. *I saved Nathalie almost forty bucks,* I thought. As we walked out of the bar, he held the door for me and my shoulder brushed against him. He stopped to pull brown leather gloves on, and I thought, *how adult,* as I shoved my hands in my coat pockets. Then he reached a gloved hand into my left pocket to fish out my hand, threaded his fingers through mine.

"You're shorter than I thought," he said. "Tiny." Men always did this—told me I was small, as if sizing me up to tuck into their trunk, as if I'd take my height as a compliment. The handholding felt exceedingly intimate, and I was relieved when he let go to push his hands through my hair and kiss me. It lasted five seconds, and his lips were warm and soft. Then he kept walking, and I followed. I wasn't so much attracted to him as I was attracted to the idea of this being an experiment; I wanted to see what it was like to follow a strange person home. Normally, I was too scared of what might happen to me to go home with someone I didn't know. None of my roommates would have noticed my disappearance for days, and they all distrusted the police, like me. But Nathalie would know what to do if she woke up and I wasn't there. She'd find me and figure out how to notify my parents. Somehow, thinking about who would find my thrown-away body made me feel better about entering a strange man's house, that ever-present threat negotiated before I walked in the door.

"White wine, right?" he asked. "I have a bottle in the fridge I can open."

The forethought of keeping a bottle of wine in the fridge, a kind he didn't drink—I wondered about that. His apartment was clean and nondescript, a row of brushed-steel appliances. Mail was scattered on the kitchen island and a coffeepot sat with its handle out. Big living room neatly arranged, blankets folded on the back of the couch. Photos under magnets on the fridge. Two bathrooms. "Where did you go to college?" I asked him. "Georgetown," he said. I looked at the time on the stove like it was a drug—it was late. Normally, I'd be alone in my bedroom, reading or looking at my phone. But I was standing here, in a strange kitchen, accepting a glass of wine.

24

New York City, 2014

"There you are. You got in late last night, huh? Do you know where the extra plastic bags are?"

Ethan was walking around in pajamas at 1:00 PM when he found me in the kitchen. His presence changed what I'd so carefully memorized about the house and its patterns. Hours that would have been silent were punctured by his presence, as he banged through the cabinets looking for the cereal or the spoons or the largest bowl. Since Nathalie couldn't work in her office, she wasn't home as much, and I missed her soft-scented presence and her pillowy steps. If I was a room away, he'd ask me where things were, and at first I liked this, him ceding to the fact that I knew where things were, that I was the one who lived here. But then I heard him asking the housekeeper the same things. "Donna, where do they keep the tea? I'm off of coffee today." The same tone of voice as when he spoke to me, asking me where the remote was, where they stored their umbrellas or Tupperware, and, currently, if they had any extra plastic bags.

"We use those bags under the sink for groceries," I said. "The reusable ones."

"But what if I want a one-use bag? What if I want to throw it out when I'm done?"

I had been fixing myself an egg and an avocado to eat before I went to get Bijou. I sliced through the soft green flesh with a knife and pinched salt and pepper on top, my back to him. I could feel him still waiting for my response.

"I don't know, buy your own disposable razor at Duane Reade and then keep the disposable bag?"

Ethan personified my confusion with the world. Was I on edge, or was he an asshole? Everyone else seemed to like him. Why did everything always feel like it was in my head?

Something about what I'd done last night made me feel safer being rude to Ethan. I'd left Andrew's at midnight in a cab he called for me, in bed by twelve thirty. It hadn't even been that late. I couldn't see him again—he thought I had a real job, that I was someone different. Still, I'd come out of my experiment alive, arrived home safe. I'd enjoyed it even, surprised myself. As the elevator took me up, I remembered a time when a man had followed me home from a late-night diner, how I'd watched him exit the cab behind me, how I'd run up my building's stairs and put a kitchen knife on my nightstand, though when I woke up I realized I'd left it out so openly it was like I was offering a weapon rather than arming myself with one. *The distant past*, I'd thought cheerfully.

"Can I eat?" I said to Ethan. He was still standing there, like he expected me to fetch him a plastic bag from my pocket.

"I'm not stopping you," he said, and walked out. My solitude felt triumphant, that he'd left me to this room by myself.

25

Kent, New York, 1999

Flop, turn, river. I listened carefully, trying to learn the rules. My dad's friends were in town. Cynthia had taken Esther to her sister's, and Charlotte was four, old enough to stay. Charlotte was a little doll that I sometimes saw on weekends, chubby pink-apple cheeks, maple-syrup eyes roving about. She liked to climb up on the furniture and walk around singing, attention clinging to her like dust in air. But she had been tucked into bed for hours, asleep with her Barbie night-light glowing, and it was me, my dad, and his friends.

They were sitting at the kitchen island playing cards. I was supposed to go to bed soon, but I could never fall asleep at my dad's. I'd watch the moon shift in the sky, I'd watch the branches rustle. I'd turn from one side to the next, I'd flip my pillow back and forth. I'd tell myself I wouldn't call my mom, because last time I'd done so, she'd told my dad, and I thought I'd never be that embarrassed as long as I lived. That night, Charlotte was already in bed when my dad let me eat with his friends around the kitchen island, sitting on barstools with burgers he'd grilled outside. Then he brought out a shiny silver suitcase, flipped up the two locks, and laid it open on the kitchen table. Inside were six coils of colorful discs, red and green and white and blue, with four red dice in between, two stacks of playing cards. Poker. *Flop*, *turn*, *river*, *bluff*, *blind*, words that didn't mean anything I thought they did—they didn't mean to flop onto your bed, to turn a corner, river like a stream; they meant something else.

One of his friends said I could be on his team to start. "So it's not some family dynasty," Mark said, pulling out the chair next to him at the table. "No secret codes between you two." I imagined having a father with whom I shared a secret code. Huddling with one of my dad's grown-up friends over a spread of cards, talking conspiratorially about our next move, my spine straightened as if pulled by the overhead lights. It was even better to be this way, my dad's equal, facing off against him, rather than a charge at his elbow that he had to try to remember things about. He sat across from me and his smile crinkled in his eyes and the tops of his cheeks.

Brett got up to open the fridge, and Mark flipped our cards quickly on their stomachs. Brett pulled out the carton of orange juice from the fridge. "Can I finish this?"

My dad shrugged, sure.

"I'm going to feel like a real asshole when Charlotte asks where the juice is at breakfast," Brett said. Everyone laughed loudly while he poured the rest of the carton into a glass filled with ice and clear vodka. I smiled widely. I didn't quite understand the joke, but it was being told in front of me. Brett was spending the night here—in from the city. They all used to work there, in New York together, and my dad had been their boss.

Mark held the cards back up after Brett took his seat. "You see here?" he said, pointing to two of them. I nodded, but I didn't. The cards in our hand had to make up some sort of combination with the ones on the table. Two of our cards had matching eights, red and black. "Go ahead," he said.

"Oh," I said. "We call," and I tossed four chips in, the way I'd seen Brett do. They all crowed at the way I threw them in, my nonchalance. I looked at my feet, swinging high up from the floor.

"She's a natural," Brett said. "You never played poker?"

"She's ten," my dad said.

"Oh, you seemed *much* older to me," he replied. "Sixteen at least."

I blushed; that was my greatest dream. We continued in the circle, throwing chips in. The dealer switched each round, and my dad was dealing now. The best times with my dad were always the games, the false competition a mask to hide behind. Maybe I wanted to be older, less of a burden. I never cared if I won. It was enough for me to sit there, invited to play. "Ready?" he said, and everyone flipped their cards over. My dad and Mark groaned, and Brett whooped and scooped the chips toward his chest, using two hands like shovels. I pouted, for show.

"This fucking—oh, sorry." Mark looked at my dad, wincing. "This freaking guy, I swear he changes his tell just to—mess with us." His mouth had hovered over the *fff* sound again before he said *mess.* I looked carefully at the table.

"I'm a good bluffer, what can I say. Otherwise I wouldn't be here," Brett said, leaning back in his chair.

"Why not?" I asked. Sometimes I just floated along on the waves of their conversation, but sometimes I wanted to know more. Everyone was open, more talkative tonight, like their mouths had been greased and couldn't help but spill out words. There was less furtive eye contact than usual, the way grown-ups always looked at each other and measured how much they could say.

"Well, I may have stretched the truth when interviewing for your dad."

Mark coughed. "Overtly lied."

"And he hired me. And it never mattered! But he wouldn't have hired me with no experience, if I'd told the truth."

I nodded seriously.

"What are you saying to my daughter?" my dad said, and with an open palm hit the back of Brett's head. I felt crowned, special: *look at them fighting over what wisdom to give me.* He turned to me. "Lying is bad. Obviously."

"I didn't say lie," Brett said. "I said bluff."

They had been saying that word, *bluff,* all night. It conjured an image of a thick paintbrush, short and stout with bristles that you'd wipe over something, the truth maybe, with brush-strokes that didn't quite cover the shape underneath. Maybe it was like a white lie. I didn't want to ask too many questions, lest I break the spell and they realize I didn't belong here.

"You should only bluff if you are prepared for the life it brings you," my dad said. "You bluff, then you can't go back."

I tried to squeeze my brain around his words. I didn't understand them, but that I might someday. I held the image in the front of my mind: my dad, eyes creased with a smile, his real daughter asleep upstairs, the words he spoke just for me.

"Okay, Willa, training wheels off!" Brett said. He pushed over a tiny stack, five chips. "I'll donate to your independence."

"Whoa, whoa, only if she wants to," my dad said, but without conviction. I could tell he was curious, like he wanted me to do it. I looked between the three of them, and they were all waiting for me. So I took the five chips and scooted my chair away from Mark.

"I don't know if I remember all the cards," I said, but they didn't seem to hear. Mark was dealing. I tried to remember what cards had won. There had been one round where my dad had two tens, and one where he won with a single jack. This last time, Brett's had looked like a jumble of numbers. A lot of times everyone just gave up and whoever didn't give up won. I looked down at my chips: I didn't know what each color meant, how much they were worth. I stacked and restacked them in three rows. My dad pushed ten over and winked. He could do that—wink—and it felt natural, a secret blessing that washed over you quick.

Mark put out three cards, and we all put in chips, and then he put out one more: a nine of hearts. I had a nine in my hand, a black one with a clover. I felt nervous—that was good. Brett scratched at his ear, and I saw Mark glance at him suspiciously. He had done that before. Brett pushed three more chips in, and so did we. Were these chips real money? I didn't know. Mark laid out the final card, a two of hearts—the river. I remembered the name of this one. I imagined something rushing, frothing, carrying baskets downstream. It was how I felt, sitting at the table with my dad and his friends. Something was carrying me along, no one had told me what to do. I had a two of diamonds. For a second I wanted to fold, to leave before they noticed. But no one folded, and we laid out our hands. My dad balled up a fist and brought it to his mouth, and when he pulled it away, he was smiling, widely, so that I saw his back teeth, the faint tracks by the corner of his eyes. "She's always been a quick learner," he said. "I knew it," and the word *always*, the words *I knew*, they felt like what happened next, which was that they all pushed their chips toward me. I had won.

26

New York City, 2014

Bijou had gotten the idea from a magazine. Last year, for her birthday, she'd taken three friends to see *The Lion King* on Broadway, but for her tenth birthday, she wanted all twelve girls in her class to come over and have a group scavenger hunt, then sleep over. Her birthday fell on a Saturday in late March and the weather forecast said it would be especially warm that week, high sixties with lots of sunshine and no chance of rain.

"We can't send a dozen girls around Manhattan without supervision, even if it is for a scavenger hunt," Nathalie said. "Maybe if we do it in teams? Like me, your dad, Willa, we each supervise, I mean, *captain* a team of a few girls?" I was in the other room, overhearing this as they planned.

Gabe made jokes about it the whole week leading up to the party—how his team was going to *smoke* Ethan's and Nathalie's. He didn't direct any of them toward me. Nathalie seemed excited, too, talking about how she was going to get her girls to come up with a team name.

"Nathalie's Nightingales," she mused one evening at the dinner table. "Nathalie's Navigators, Nathalie's Ninjas!"

"Nathalie's Nitwits," Gabe teased. "*Ohhhh*!"

"Nincompoops," Ethan said. They looked at me.

Nymphos was the word that almost sprung off my tongue. I couldn't think of anything else. Sex had been on my mind ever since I'd had it, and I had to push it away.

"*Mom*," Bijou said. "The team isn't about *you*."

*

Twelve girls were coming over, and I braced for invasion. Six were sleeping over later, and I imagined skipping over little-girl limbs in the morning. Bijou seemed so grown up on her own, and when she was with Skylar, they were polite and quiet, but in a group, it was a lot of squealing.

Bijou had planned activities for the entire evening. She'd even written out little schedules, like curlicue menus, to be distributed to each guest. First, they would go on the neighborhood scavenger hunt—Bijou had allotted two hours for this. Then, they'd have dinner back at the apartment; then, ice-cream-sundae-making time; then, makeovers; then, a movie and sleepover in the living room for those who were staying. Some of the girls' parents didn't let them have sleepovers. Ethan was heading out after the scavenger hunt to stay at a friend's. I wished I could as well, and I couldn't tell exactly how long I was expected to be on duty. No one had told me, and it seemed unkind to ask. Of course I cared about Bijou's birthday, but I would have enjoyed it more if it were just the family. And when I worked more hours than usual, they only sometimes remembered to adjust my pay; Nathalie sent me two payments a month, and unless I reminded her, she'd forget to add or subtract.

Girls and their parents streamed in, dropping off gift bags and wrapped presents in the foyer, kissing Nathalie on the cheek and relaying dietary restrictions. Ethan sat on the carpeted floor while Bijou's friends looked swooningly at him, asking him questions. I remembered having a crush on my babysitter's boyfriend when I was a kid, tearing out photos of Devon Sawa and Jonathan Taylor Thomas. It occurred to me that they were exactly who Ethan looked like.

Eventually Bijou had decided that it was most fair for her not to choose the groups beforehand and for the names to be picked out of a hat. I ended up with Bijou's two Asian friends: an Indian girl with bangs and a mixed Japanese girl with hair that was almost blonde. "Well, we're probably the smartest team, aren't we?" I said, out of having nothing to say, and then felt horrified for saying. "I'm Willa, what are your names again?" There was also a brunette with pigtail braids and freckles. Each of us had a team of three girls, except for Gabe, who also had Bijou. The scavenger hunt was more like a photo hunt: each team had to take Polaroid photos of each of the fifteen items on the list, and whoever finished them all first, won. *A pigeon,* was one. *Someone with an odd hairstyle. The fire station where* Ghostbusters *was filmed. Latte art—but you're not allowed to buy your own latte!*

"Well, looks like someone got the smartest team, huh?" Ethan whispered to me as we left.

*

They trooped ahead of me to do the latte-art one. "We'll ask someone to take the lid off their coffee!" the pigtailed girl yelled. "Wait up," I said softly, trying to get more in the mood. I had woken up a bit prickly, and everything was irritating me. I was holding the Polaroid camera; Nathalie had bought four for the party, each in a pastel shade, and ours was a mint green. I wondered if they'd notice if I kept it. When I caught up to the girls, they were inside the coffee shop, sweetly asking a customer waiting for her latte if we could take a picture of it. "Sorry," I said to her, but she held out her cup willingly. I aimed the camera down. The foam was arranged in an uneven heart.

"Maybe I'll get a quick coffee," I said to the girls. "Hold on a second."

"Can we take the camera and wait outside then? Maybe we'll see a pigeon," Mari said. I handed over the camera and got in line. *Why am I a nanny, again?* I thought as I watched the barista who was making the latte-art, who appeared blissfully silent and untalked-to in contrast to the one taking orders from customers. I had been there before. I had hated that too.

It took a while for me to get my own latte, but I looked out the window, checking to see if I could spot the tallest girl, the one with the pigtails, periodically. But when I got outside, it was just her. "They followed a pigeon into the park over there."

"What?" I said to her. "And you let them?"

She looked taken aback. "I stayed so I could tell you—"

I took her wrist. There was a tiny park across the street from the coffee shop, an enclosed patch of benches and daffodils, and maybe they were at the entrance. "Which way?" I asked. The pigtailed girl—I thought her name was Hannah—pointed. We circled the perimeter and didn't see them. My heart jumped into my throat. As if it wouldn't have been bad enough for me to lose Bijou, I was going to lose her friends.

"What were they wearing? Do you remember?"

"Ridhi was wearing a denim jacket, I think. Mari had on pink?"

"Okay, I'm sure they're over here waiting for us, no need to panic," I said.

"Oh, there's a pigeon!" Hannah said. Her upbeat tone made me think for an instant she'd seen the girls, but she was looking at a cluster of pigeons pecking at bread crumbs. There were a million pigeons in this city all the time. How did they think they needed to go seek one out? What if Nathalie saw the girls without me? What if Bijou did? She would tell Nathalie. What if—?

"Oh my God," I said through my teeth.

"Where should we look now?" Hannah said cheerfully.

"Don't you watch the news?" I hissed. "Why would you let them go off like that?"

She paused. "What do you mean, the news?"

I couldn't decide which way they would have gone. I circled the faux park again. I looked down the street past the coffee shop. No, I would have seen them through the windows. I took a chance and walked one way, but after two blocks, nothing. I circled back to the park and took another street, Hannah trailing behind me. Images flashed through my head: Nathalie kneeling down and holding them in her arms, shaking her head at me; Bijou crying because her birthday was ruined since her friends had obviously been kidnapped and killed; Ethan raising his eyebrow at me as I packed my things to leave the apartment; the newspaper clippings, the headlines. What would people say? Would my parents find out? I'd had all this time to become a better nanny, to learn how you should pay attention to kids, and all I'd done was learn to poach an egg and give Bijou food poisoning once. Maybe it wasn't the world's fault that there wasn't a place for me. Maybe it was my fault for never trying. For waiting for things to come to me as naturally as they seemed to arrive for everyone else. Maybe I thought I shouldn't have to try if no one else did. But what did it matter how I got there, if I got there? What did it matter if I didn't mean to lose the kids, if they ended up lost?

"Should I text them?" Hannah said.

"You can text them? Yes, yes, text them, text them."

They were one block away, photographing an English bulldog, like the scavenger hunt sheet said to.

"Hey, you two!" Mari said. "We've already gotten three things!"

I tried to smile brightly. I wondered how I could persuade them not to include this part of the adventure in any retellings later.

*

After the ice cream sundaes, the girls dispersed into the living room to do their makeovers. Nathalie had laid out towels on the floor around makeup castles and piles of clothes.

"Well, that's my cue," Ethan said, pulling his jacket from the closet. "I hope you ladies have fun!"

"You're not staying?" one of the more brash ones pouted. I couldn't remember so many names.

"Oh, I wish I could, Kimmy," he said, smiling. I stood, too, went to grab my purse from the entryway and take it into my room, where I planned to pour myself a large glass of my screw-top sauvignon blanc and lie in bed.

"I heard your team had quite the drama today," Ethan said. He smiled devilishly and acted like he was zipping his lips. I ignored him and took my bag from the hook. "Hey, what are you doing now?" he asked.

I could practically see myself twisting off the cap, pouring a cup to the brim. "Going to read in my room for a bit."

"Want to get a drink? My treat. My friend's party isn't for a couple of hours."

I hesitated, but in the end the pull of a cocktail someone else had made, even an hour stolen in the real person's world, was too strong. I sat in my room drinking twelve-dollar wine almost every night, watching the walls like they were closing in on me. I wanted fresh air. I agreed, looking quickly at Nathalie. She looked up and waved at us, then looked back at Bijou. We got in the elevator.

"Just for an hour," I said.

"Is there a bar you like around here?" he asked, though he had taken a sharp left out of the front door, already leading us somewhere.

I'd never gone to any bar around here. "Monique is nice," I said, "but it's a bit of a walk." He said he had one he liked down the street, and there were two empty stools as soon as he pushed open the door.

"Bijou seems better," he said, once we had gotten our drinks.

"Better than what?"

"Oh. Never mind."

"You can't just say that," I said. "Now you have to tell me."

"Well, after our mom died . . ." I looked away at the mention of his mom. I had lost every opportunity to say *I'm sorry* about her death, and never knew when to jam it in. Did you still say *I'm sorry* if it had been years, and you'd just found out? "You know how Nat's not that maternal?" he said. I stared at him; Nathalie was perfect. "Like, all business and distance, and hugs when she has the time for it. Nathalie's exactly our dad. A nice pat on the head on your birthday. Our mom was different. Clumsy, funny. She liked dirty jokes. Obsessed with Bee. She's the one who made Bee an insufferable little snob when it comes to cooking. They literally would make like, lasagna and coq au vin when Bee was five."

"That's sweet," I said, though my stomach soured. I saw Bijou as if carved from crystal, turning a shadowy side toward the light.

"Yeah, like, after our mom died, Nathalie kept finding Band-Aids on her. But she could never find any scrapes. She said they were cooking wounds. It didn't last too long, but I felt like Nat kind of brushed over it too quickly."

I sipped my drink stoically, imagining Bijou, her serious face, her particular hands, unpeeling a Band-Aid and sticking it to her unblemished skin. I thought of her applying the pressure to make it stick, pressing each corner down. I thought of that sharp smack when you pulled it away from skin.

"But she seems better?" I asked.

He shrugged. "Does she seem better to you?"

I hadn't known there was something to improve from, I thought. I hadn't even been looking.

27

New York City, 2014

Nathalie was going to London for a week, and Gabe had a conference in Boston. The first night Nathalie was gone, I went into her closet, like an afterthought. Bijou was in the kitchen filling a pot with water to boil. I slid open one of the doors and stuck my arm in, as if I were hot and it was an icebox. I swept my fingers up and down the row, feeling silks and stretchy jersey and the drag of sewn-on crystals. Then I slid the door shut and walked out. I walked back into the kitchen, and Bijou looked up. I smiled back at her cleanly. I looked down at the counter, where she'd laid out ingredients.

"What are we making again?" I asked. I had felt extra delicate around Bijou in the kitchen since Ethan talked to me, had offered to try any outlandish recipe she wanted. The day after her birthday party, I'd even asked if she knew how to make lasagna. She had looked at me curiously before telling me yes.

She gave me instructions when we cooked, even if we were both reading the recipe. She used to make me do the chopping and anything with oil, but along the way the rules had softened, and often she did those, too. I must have been deemed responsible by Nathalie at some point offstage. Usually I moved around behind Bijou, wiping drops of olive oil or collecting the discarded skins of onion and putting them in the trash.

"Can you chop the sausage? And then the peppers?" she asked.

"Here you go," I said, placing the cutting board to the right of the stove. There were spots next to the stove for the expensive olive oil and the cooking olive oil, little crocks of sea salt and red pepper flakes, and a large silver pepper grinder. There were also three types of vinegar, red wine and two balsamic, that we never used. I picked them up and placed them back in the cabinet; it looked neater this way. "What do you miss about her?" I said, but then Ethan walked in.

"Moving things around?" he said.

"You know, you walk very quietly. I can't ever hear when you're coming." He seemed to take this as a compliment, so I added, "It's disturbing." I put my head down to slice through the peppers, one red, one yellow. They spilled out little white seeds that stuck to my skin.

"I'm stealthy like that," he said, sliding lazily into a stool behind the counter. "What are you making, Bee?"

I hated that he called her Bee, too, even though the nickname existed before I did.

"Pad thai with shrimp and sausage," she said.

"Is that your recipe?" Ethan said, looking to me.

"I'm not Thai." I meant the words to come out pointedly, poisoned, but they sounded deflated, mechanical.

"Oh, what are you then?" he asked.

"I'm Chinese, remember." I was embarrassed to sound so docile around Bijou, annoyed that Ethan forgot. I took a breath in and spoke again, to change the subject. "Ethan," I said, trying a new way to bring his mom in. I wanted Bee to be able to talk. "What was your favorite thing to eat, growing up? Nathalie told me it was her—I mean, your mom's roast chicken."

"Mmmm, with the rosemary skin. Nat never ate the skin. Skin is the best part."

"So that was your favorite too?"

"No. I liked it when she made meatloaf."

"Meatloaf?" It was such a normal thing.

"And I'd put globs of cold, cold ketchup on it." He leaned into Bijou. "Your mom is terrible at making meatloaf, you know. You should ask her for it."

"You're obsessed with whatever Nathalie is bad at," I said. "Plus she makes turkey meatloaf all the time."

"Yeah, but is it good?"

"I mean, yeah, it's good. It's healthy."

"Good and healthy aren't the same, contrary to popular Adrien belief," he said. "But I'm a Parker."

The pan hissed as Bijou moved things around in it. I picked something up and set it down. She asked me to watch the pan while she went to use the bathroom, and I took over her position near the stove but didn't stir. She'd only asked me to watch.

"What's your favorite thing from growing up?" he asked me. I looked at him quizzically. "What? You asked me. Only you're allowed to know about the other person's family?"

"I didn't say that," I said. "Um . . . sometimes, my mom made blueberry pancakes." I was glad to have my back to him, and I picked up the wooden spoon and stirred the sausages around, looked at their blackened marks. My mom made thin-flat pancakes with deep-blue splotches, the outer edges gone lacy with crisp. Not pretty pancakes, not airy and thick like on television commercials, but I preferred them to the ones at IHOP topped with whipped cream and berries pummeled to syrup. My mom and her sweet tooth wanted chocolate chips in them, but for me and my acid-hungry tongue, she made them with blueberries. We could make them when no one had shopped for weeks; all you needed were staples and a scoop of the blueberries she kept in the freezer. We ate them at the kitchen table with thick squares of butter and waterfalls of syrup.

"I haven't had pancakes in forever," he said. "We'd have them on Sundays before church, growing up." There were times, when he spoke to me normally, or when we had a satisfying sort of banter, that I enjoyed his presence. That I did think: *Wouldn't it be easier for me if we were friends?* What would convince Nathalie to keep me forever like one more person in her family warming to me?

Bijou came back in and I surrendered the pan to her. What I liked best about my mom's pancakes was that after we ate them, our teeth would turn blue. Not the blue of Smurfs and sky, but a gritty black-blue, as if our teeth had decayed together. We ate them and bared our teeth in the mirror, where we matched in our mouths' purple dye, like we were both, finally, the same.

*

Ethan left while Bijou and I were eating. Dinner, then a party—he stayed out late, two in the morning sometimes. Bijou was in bed and it was only eight o'clock. I stood in the center of the apartment and spun in a small circle. *I'm not done talking for the evening. I don't want to be done yet.* I'd thought being inside a house full of people and voices and rhythms would cure me of loneliness, but sometimes it made it worse because I was contained. Bijou went to bed, and I couldn't leave the house. I walked through the living room and touched each picture frame, each knickknack standing on display. A paperweight in the shape of a globe. A letter opener that gleamed a darkened gold. The bottles in the bar cart, green for gin and clear for vodka and whiskey that glowed like tiger's eye. I thought about drinking, to pass the time. I looked at the time and wondered if Ethan would be home soon, but no, he'd left only an hour ago. He was going to Williamsburg, and trying to make a point of taking the subway everywhere, as if it were impressive, so he wouldn't be home for hours. Donna would be here in the morning. I'd follow behind her and she'd tell me about her kids and her walking group. There was an open bottle of red wine on the countertop, cork sticking out. It was three-quarters full. I poured myself a glass and walked back out.

I thought about turning on the TV, and I walked right next to it, considering. As if someone were watching me do it, as if I'd had a quick idea, I kept walking, into Nathalie and Gabe's bedroom. I turned on the light in the bathroom and looked at all of Nathalie's instruments for beauty. I turned on the faucet to wash my face. A secret: sometimes the water took forever to get warm in rich people's bathrooms too. I drank wine and waited. I uncapped lids and left them askew. I opened the lipsticks and unscrewed them to the top. I picked up the toner and soaked a cotton ball through with so much liquid that it dripped off onto my lap. "Shit," I said, wiping at the stain on my jeans. It was an old pair that I wore because they were comfortable enough to sit around in, but I didn't like the whiskered fade around the thighs, or the awkward length they hit at my ankles. The toner seeped through the denim, cold and creeping, and I stood up with a start. I unbuttoned the jeans and kicked them off around my feet. I walked back out, into Nathalie's closet. Donna had left a pair of her jeans in my laundry the week before, and I'd given them back. I wondered where Nathalie had put them.

I opened her closet doors fully, swung open all four cabinets and stared at it all. Then I saw this dress that Nathalie had worn to a gala, months earlier. She'd looked so stunning in it, it was embarrassing for her, Bijou and I breathing out compliments as she gathered items for her clutch and told us to stop. It was a moss green, an emerald with the light gone out, a floor-length skirt and a cap-sleeved, beaded bodice, buttons all the way down the back from shoulder blades to hip bones. It was the buttons that got me. They were little gemstones sewn on so delicately, fitting into their tiny loops. Without thinking, as fast as I could, I tore off the rest of my clothes, my underwear remaining, and held the dress in front of me, wondering how to wriggle my way in. I stepped inside, fluttering it up my body, snaking my arms through the tiny sleeves. My hair was darker than Nathalie's, my skin was darker, yes, but the color, it still looked good on me. I turned away from the mirror and looked over my shoulder, concentrating on fastening up the back. The gemstones were so small; my fingers were trembling. I'd take it right off afterward. I got to the top of the dress and turned around to face the mirror. I took the skirt in my hands and swished it softly around my feet, standing on my tiptoes as if in heels. Clothes like this *felt* different, creamy like butter, soft against your skin.

I wanted to take a picture of myself—I wanted proof that I looked like this. I gathered my hair in my hands and pulled it off my neck into a low bun; that was how Nathalie had worn it. I walked into the bathroom to get my phone, and saw the water was still running. The bathroom light was brighter; the dress looked more emerald, less moss, in this room, against the black-tiled backdrop. I pinched it between two fingers, rubbing back and forth, when suddenly—*ding*. The elevator.

My mind went instantly blank. I felt frozen, then jolted. I had to get this off. I began furiously unbuttoning, and I heard the elevator doors close. Ethan was home. I counted the buttons I was freeing: *one, two, three, four, five,* even though I hadn't counted how many there were. My jeans were still here, on the tile, but my shirt—it was out there, the closet was open, the hanger was on the floor.

"Willa?" he said.

I slammed Nathalie's bathroom door shut. "Ethan?" I responded dumbly, as if surprised.

I heard his footsteps in the hallway. I heard him pick up the hanger and drop it on the floor. I finished unbuttoning, but my plan was flawed, because there was no top in here for me to put on.

"What are you doing in there?"

"My bathroom—I ran out of tampons," I said, grateful for whatever synapse had fired to put that word on my tongue. "I came in here to borrow one." I could see the shadows of his shoes through the door. He should have taken them off.

"Did you know your shirt's out here?"

"I was hot. I didn't think anyone was home. Shouldn't you be out?" I flushed the toilet, just to make noise. "Can we talk when I'm done?"

"I'll be outside," he said smoothly. I could hear his smirk through the door. With tingling hands, I pulled off the dress. I folded it up as small as it could go and looked around me. The bottom left drawer under the sink looked wide—I shoved the dress in there. My jeans were still wet from the toner, but I pulled them back on, so I was wearing jeans and a black bra in Nathalie's bathroom. I wished I had taken the picture. I washed my hands, for some reason. Then I pulled the door open and peeked my head out before grabbing for my shirt to pull over my head. I walked out and tried to look unruffled. Ethan was sitting at the dining room table, his feet up in polka-dot socks, flipping through a *New Yorker*.

"Want a glass of wine?" he said. "I took this from Gabe's stash."

"I don't think so," I said. I remembered I'd left my glass of wine in Nathalie's bathroom as well.

"Oh, it's okay," he said. "I talked to Nat on the phone today like I always do. She told me I could."

"Aren't you supposed to be at a party?"

"Sometimes I find my friends really dull. They're stuck in college. So I came back here. I thought you must be bored all by yourself. It's lonely in here."

I paused. When Ethan wasn't around, I knew I couldn't trust him. But when faced with him, I wondered why I was so defensive. Maybe he didn't mean me any harm. Maybe he really thought I was lonely.

"Have you recovered from your hot flash?"

"So where did you go tonight?" I said, ignoring him. He'd already poured me a glass, so I picked it up.

"I actually didn't. I walked around. I wasn't in the mood. Had a drink at Acqua and decided to come back. What did *you* do tonight?"

I squeezed the glass in my hand, wondered if I could break it. "Pad thai. Dishes. I was just cleaning up. Going to read in my room a little."

"What were you doing in there?" he asked.

"I told you. I needed a tampon."

"In Nat's bathroom? Topless?"

"Ethan. I know, it's kind of weird, I was just feeling itchy, pulled it off for like one second. Have you never walked around shirtless? And like, sorry for menstruating. I needed a tampon." I was conscious that he was using few words, that I was overexplaining. I looked at him pleadingly.

"I never noticed you have freckles under your eyes," he said.

I brought my hand to my cheek without meaning to. "Yeah," I said.

"I've been wondering. What's next for you? After this?"

What *after*? What *next*?

"What are you planning to do with your life?"

"This." I stared into the glass. Who knew what I meant—the wine, the laziness, the childcare.

"I like that," he said. "That you don't care."

I looked up at him sharply. "That's not what I said. At all."

"God, all right; you're so sensitive. So what do you care about?"

"What do *you* care about?" I hated being called sensitive, though I was.

"I care about books, I care about school, I care about my family, I'm almost finished with my doctorate, and then I'll have to care about getting a job."

"And an apartment," I added.

He looked at me. "Perhaps."

"Don't you—or didn't you—have a job? I thought you were a professor," I said. Trying.

I saw a glimmer of sheepishness, but he recovered quickly. "I was adjuncting. I still could." He let the words hang. "I don't know if I really want to teach anymore. It's probably like, you used to want to be a therapist, and now you don't."

"I didn't want to be a therapist," I said. Perhaps I had for a second, but Ethan didn't know that.

"But didn't you study psychology?"

"Well yeah, but I mean, lots of people study psychology. It's like English. It's just interesting."

"Must be nice to go to school for what's *interesting*," he said. "My dad almost cut me off when I switched from econ."

"Oh, you're so oppressed."

"It must be nice to be so free, is all."

"And it must be nice to be so coddled."

We stared at each other evenly. "I wake up at six to take Bijou to school." I could feel an apology forming, a habit of wanting to make up for my leaving, but I resisted, and instead gave him a small, wordless smile.

"Okay then," he said. He scratched behind his ear. "Good night."

I got into bed and tried to think about what he'd seen earlier as if I were an objective onlooker. I felt like it was hard, sometimes, to tell what was normal and what wasn't because I didn't have anyone to talk to. But my excuse was okay, wasn't it? Strange, yes, that I'd done it, that my shirt had been on the floor, but could Nathalie blame me if I'd actually needed a tampon? If I'd walked around partially undressed for five minutes? For some reason, I felt like he wouldn't tell her. I changed into pajamas, I brushed my teeth, and I brought the sheets up to my neck. I set my alarm for 3:00 AM, and when it went off, I was still awake, waiting. I tiptoed out into the hallway and then delicately rehung the dress, went into the bathroom, screwed on all the caps, cleaned off the counters—tried my best to erase it all.

28

New York City, 2014

When Nathalie came back, she slept for a day, and woke up like she'd missed being a mom, picking out activities for Bijou. I was in the kitchen cutting Granny Smith apples into slices when Nathalie told me I would have Friday off.

Ethan perked up at this. I saw him open his mouth and then close it, as if thinking. "Friday. Friday I have this thing," Ethan said. He smiled innocently. "Willa, I had been meaning to ask you if you had plans."

I looked at Nathalie quickly, hoping to be saved. But she only reached over and brushed a bread crumb off the corner of his mouth.

"Well . . ." Should I say that I was getting sick, that I was feeling tired? "Obviously no," I finally said. "I thought I was working."

It was his friend's engagement party. Nathalie smiled widely. "Oh, won't that be sweet. That's so kind of you to invite her."

I felt as if I were Donna, when Gabe gave her Mets tickets he'd gotten at work. "How did your son like the game?" I remembered Nathalie asking the next week. I remembered seeing Donna hesitate before going into an elaborately grateful anecdote. I remembered I already knew the script.

*

Cutting out rent made me feel responsible, self-sufficient, proud of how my bank account had swelled, and didn't that mean that I deserved a treat? This was what I told myself when I bought myself things. I'd seen a dress in a nearby window display and thought, *Wouldn't that look nice on me?* I knew I'd have nowhere to wear it, but I bought it anyway.

On Friday, I put it on in my room. The dress was a silvery-gray satin slip that I liked for how much it looked like pajamas, effortless and intimate. It had thin straps and reached below my knees, with a slit up one leg. It was an April evening just warm enough to wear it with black tights and a jacket. I put a long strand of fake pearls on, tied it once around my neck like a choker. I thought it looked casually glam, in a twenties way.

Ethan looked handsome, I thought grudgingly. He'd put on charcoal-gray slacks and a white button-down shirt. Gabe watched us leave with his mouth in a straight line. I felt as if we were in the kind of sitcom where the kids leave for prom, and the dad disapproves.

"Behave," was the last thing Gabe said before we left.

"You hear that?" Ethan said as he moved to push the button for the lobby.

I pulled at the sleeves on my jacket. "He wasn't talking to me."

"I like your dress," he said.

"Thank you," I heard myself say, like a child, prim and surprised.

*

When we arrived to his friend's Chelsea apartment, I saw that all the girls were in jeans. Red lips and long black eyelashes, high-waisted jeans exposing a two-finger slice of creamy skin. Most of them were blonde, too, but more immediately, I noticed that all of these thin, moisturized, toned women were wearing tight dark denim, and I was wearing a shapeless dress. I'd allowed myself to feel pretty earlier while getting ready in my room, but I wanted to pull the pearls off and coil them away in my purse. I thought about hissing to Ethan, *Why didn't you tell me to dress more casually?* But I didn't want him to win. I tried not to slouch. There had to be someone else in a dress.

"Jacket?" Ethan reached behind my collar, his hands warm on my neck. I flinched and shook my head. I wanted to keep it on. It hid how much of my shoulders would be exposed if he took it off.

He handed his coat to the coat check attendant and motioned to the bar. I looked around the room, watching the women. It reminded me of being in high school, at a party I was too young for, and observing the older girls with reverence. I was too afraid to speak to them, so I'd stand there and watch. I wanted to know how they became so beautiful but jagged in the right places, tough and accepted. They were all dimples and laughter but seemed like they could slice a hand that touched them the wrong way. I would hear words they said and slip them into my brain for later, to roll them around on my tongue. I'd watch how they kept their cigarettes in their waistbands and broke tabs off their beer cans and strung them into bracelets. I watched all this and I tried to do it, but it never worked for me. Everyone knew I was pretending to be someone else. I watched the women around me. Their earlobes hung heavy with gold, their false eyelashes fluttered prettily, and they knew where to hold their hands. But I didn't feel the way I used to—that I'd give anything to become one of them. They'd see through me, and that was worse. I would have to be myself. Ethan came up beside me and handed me a glass of champagne. "I hate champagne," I told him.

He raised an eyebrow. "What does the princess want?"

I saw someone nearby drinking a martini, so I said that.

"But of course." He took the flute away from me and drained it in one sip, his Adam's apple bulging.

"Dirty," I clarified. "And vodka." I thought gin was too flowery. "And actually, I can take off my coat." I shimmied my arms out and waited to see if he would take it from me.

"I'll have one too," he said, folding my jacket onto his forearm. Once he turned, I smiled to myself. When he came back, I took a large sip, the salty brine flooding my mouth. Maybe I didn't like vodka anymore.

"Perfect," I said, eyeing my glass full of pond water. I pulled out the stick of olives and bit the closest one off.

"The elusive girl likes martinis," he said. "One more fact to collect."

"I'm not elusive." I regretted it as soon as I said it; I wanted to be.

"What's your favorite color?" he said.

"Green."

"Who's your favorite musician?"

"Bowie," I said, though I hadn't been listening to music that much anymore, inside their house. Ethan teetered off to the side of the room, and I instinctively moved too. "Don't you have, um, friends here you want to talk to?" I took another sip. "Where's your friend who's getting engaged?"

Ethan shrugged. "Do you ever hate your friends?"

I held my glass tightly, waiting for him to point out that I really didn't have any, that I didn't leave the apartment that much. He swept the room with his eyes and then turned back to me. He took another sip and waited.

"I have trouble finding the right people, I think."

"Yeah. I need to find other people. These ones—dull. But you know. It's like, the friends you go to college with or you grow up with, you end up being tied to them."

"You must like something about them. The history, at least."

He pursed his lips and a dimple appeared.

"I grew away from my college friends too," I admitted. "I can't find anything to talk to them about."

"So do you like being a nanny?"

I finished my martini and looked around for a place to set it down. Ethan motioned to an end table closer to the wall, and I moved to put it down. He followed and leaned against the wall. I saw him catch someone's eye, and I expected a friend of his to come over, but instead it was a tray with more martinis on it, and he plucked two off.

"Thank you," I said to the server, though I noticed he hadn't. "I do like it sometimes. There's variety. I do a lot of different things with Bijou. It's fun. She's so great. I get to live in Tribeca. So many other jobs, you have to care about fifty people at the same time. It's nice to focus on one person."

"On Bijou," he said.

I nodded. Obviously.

"Or did you mean Nathalie? Oh fuck," he said suddenly. "I cannot see him tonight." He turned his back to the crowd, boxing me in against the wall, so I was the only one who could see his face, and everyone else could see his blond swirl of hair, the nape of his neck. I started laughing, he looked so nervous, and he looked at me and smiled as his cheeks reddened.

"Well, cheers to hiding," he said, holding the edge of his glass up, and we drank. This one was with gin, and I liked it better. I hoped Ethan would forget that I'd asked for vodka. He placed it on the table behind me after a sip, and his hands brushed mine. He coughed and moved a step away, his face reddening further. For a second I thought about it. Of course I did. What was the best-case scenario? That Ethan and I ended up together. We'd begin to date and eventually I'd sit at every dinner with him and the Adriens, Ethan refilling my glass when it got low. We'd go out to dinner at restaurants with white tablecloths and dessert carts, drinking cocktails before bottles of wine with no thoughts of the prices next to them. My ring would be huge, it would have to be, one of those ones that hung to the side on my small finger. Bijou would be—my niece. Imagine the stories we would tell, how I had interviewed one day with Nathalie and been so unremarkable. We'd laugh about the origin story. I'd be at Bijou's high school graduation, her college one. I would figure out how to ask about her grandmother. My life wouldn't hinge so much on my own decisions, Ethan's familial wealth like a feathered mattress that would always break my fall.

I hadn't had that much liquor in months, and I felt like my senses were covered in tulle, dramatic and scratchy. I saw this vision, how much it would solve things for me, but I also thought of how quickly Ethan pivoted, how he seemed nice one second and murderous the next. How the day I'd met him, he handed me his coat. I squirmed my shoulders a bit to the left, so I was standing a few more inches away, and he turned so he was more open to the room. Almost immediately, a couple ran up to him, a girl throwing her arms around his neck briefly, and her boyfriend slapping his back. Then they turned to me.

"Katie, right?"

I shook my head slowly, looking at Ethan. He scratched the back of his head briefly. "This is Willa. Willa—Kristen, Joe."

"Oh, I'm so sorry—" she faltered. "I've had too much champagne! Um, Willa, so nice to meet you. Do you live around here?"

I wondered where they thought Ethan lived. "Tribeca," I finally said. I looked at Ethan. I knew what it meant to be mistaken for someone else in a room full of white people.

"Oh, cool," she said. "I live in the West Village, but I love Tribeca. How do you two know each other?"

"She works for my sister," Ethan said. "Nathalie. That's how we met."

That's how we met seemed so personal, as if it were a time we had transcended, a story we told. The one I'd been imagining, but from his mouth I didn't like it.

"Mm-hmm," I intoned. "How do you all know each other? College?"

"I went to Princeton, yeah, a year below him," Kristen said. "Joe went to Brown. Nathalie's so cool." She tipped up the last sip of her champagne. "I met her once. She must be fun to work for. Where is she again—Morgan Stanley?"

I waited a second to see if Ethan would break in, but then when he opened his mouth, I decided to. "I'm her nanny," I said crisply, enunciating the word.

"Oooooh," Kristen said, her mouth round, then pursed, then back to normal. She was wearing red lipstick that was fading toward the center. That always happened to me. "I babysat in college too. I *love* kids. How old is Nathalie's?"

"She's ten," I said. Kristen nodded. I couldn't say she was being unkind. Her boyfriend took a sip of his drink. Ethan cleared his throat. Time seemed to stop, as if each time the conversation turned to me, there was nothing else to say. But I didn't know how much I could blame them. I didn't want to talk about nannying. I felt a sour self-hatred in my mouth. I smiled tinily up at them, my transient unruliness silenced as I drank the rest of my martini.

"How's the dissertation going, man?" Joe asked, and as I listened to Ethan lie, I felt a small kinship with him, even as I hated to stand at his side with nothing to say.

The party flashed by me. More girls in black, in white, in gold. More platform heels and denim jeans. More introductions. After what felt like hours but had been only one, I heard the tinkle of cutlery on crystal, the announcement of a speech. I felt relieved for the interruption, that we would be expected to stand silent and alert for a certain number of minutes, but then I felt Ethan close his hand around my wrist, his thumb to my pulse. He nodded to the right, and I followed him because what else would I do? There was a door to the balcony in the next room. We stepped out onto it, and the entire skyline loomed before us. Even if I lived here forever, I thought I'd always be awed by those jigsaw buildings on a clear night.

"So . . ." I said. "How's it going for you?" My feelings shifted minute to minute. I had hated him earlier, hated him for his embarrassment of me and my job, but then for some unknown reason, I felt bad for him too.

"It's boring, isn't it?"

I wasn't sure how to answer. It was hard to feel thrilled by a room full of people you didn't know, but I'd enjoyed the little salmon tartare tarts that had been passed around. "Aren't these your friends?"

"In a way." He pulled a cigarette and a red Bic lighter from his inside jacket pocket and lit it with one hand cupped. He held it out to me after he inhaled, but I shook my head.

"They all seem to work in finance," I noted.

"Just like Nathalie," he said.

"Yeah, but Nathalie's not like *that*," I said, not even sure what I meant.

He seemed to look at me quizzically. Was Nathalie like that? No, no. Nathalie was much more of a full, appealing person.

"Kill me if I end up working at a bank," he said.

"You know, Ivy League academia isn't that much more ethical than a bank," I said, grateful for the podcast I'd heard last week that had said as much.

"I don't really want academia either, though."

I moved to the balcony railing and contented myself with looking at the view. We were twenty-five stories up, and I could see the Empire State Building, lit up with blue tonight.

"What do you want to do, Willa?" He'd asked me before, but I found his voice to be different this time. Softer, sadder, a little younger. I kept my back to him. My shoulders stiffened. What if I didn't know? "Not a therapist, I know," he said lightly. "No, what did you want to be when you were a kid?"

"An actress," I said. I never told anyone that, but that was what I wanted as a kid. I was enthralled by how they could become other people so wholly for the time it took to shoot a movie. I envied that people told them what to say, who to be, and all they had to do was be that person, and not themselves. I'd tried to take an acting class once in college, but it felt so vulnerable it made my skin crawl. I hadn't thought of it in a while. "But not anymore."

"A teacher?" he asked.

I hate kids, I almost said, but then remembered myself.

"I see you as being a little artistic, though," he said. "You're always going to movies or reading or going to museums."

I didn't tell him that the museums were Bijou's idea, liking to read wasn't a career path, and yes, I liked movies, but so did everyone. "Thanks," I said, because it sounded like a compliment, and I was surprised that he had even observed me clearly enough to catalog my hobbies. But were they Bijou's hobbies or mine?

When we walked back inside, a photographer asked if he could take our picture. A hired photographer, someone with a bow tie on and a giant flash attached to his camera. Ethan put his arm around me and tugged my body into his. "What are your names?" the photographer asked.

"Ethan Parker and Willa Chen," Ethan said to him. "C-H-E-N." The photographer handed us a business card with a hyperlink on it—the website where all these photos would be.

"Fancy," I said. Ethan slipped the card into his inside jacket pocket.

We stayed for another hour before I realized that I kept sloshing my drink over its rim like I couldn't keep my hand straight. I told Ethan I wanted to leave.

"I have to be up." I heard my voice come out slushily. "I take Bijou to school."

"It's Friday," he reminded me. "And she's at a sleepover."

"I still want to go home."

To my surprise, he didn't argue but gathered our coats, finished his drink, and held his arm out for me to leave first. We slid into a cab and rode the ten minutes in silence, but not uncomfortable silence. The cabdriver was playing the radio really loud, and I felt like my stomach was sloshing with all the gin.

"Nightcap?" he said when we got up to the apartment.

I looked at him, considering. He did look like Devon Sawa; it was annoying. "I need water."

"Aww, buzzkill," he said. He went over to the bar cart and poured himself a splash of scotch. "You know, you don't get that Asian flush. Lucky."

I took off my shoes in the entryway. "Why do you have to say things like that all the time? God." I went to the kitchen and took out the sparkling water, poured it in a tall glass, and then sank into the couch. Sometimes I didn't realize how drunk I was until I came home, everything rippling. I remembered this from before. He sat too close to me, and I edged over on the cushion. He held up his hands, that gesture I'd seen before, like, *Don't make such a big deal out of it.*

That gesture—that was why I hated him, how he could do or say anything he wanted so long as he held his hands up and said he didn't mean it.

"Who's Katie?" I said.

He looked at his hands. "My ex-fiancée."

"When did you two break up?"

"Around September."

"And she looks like me?"

He shrugged. "Never thought of it. Not really. I guess a little." He turned to look at me then, and then he reached out and held my chin between his finger and thumb. "I mean, I think you're much more beautiful." He had a sweet-boy look on his face, a blond curl waving over his smooth forehead. I could feel his thumbprint sticking up into the soft part under my mouth—it wasn't gentle, it was like a hook. I wasn't breathing. Was he really this close to my face? I felt immobile. Then he sat back and sipped his scotch. I drank my sparkling water but felt the room had changed. It felt familiar, lit up with the charge of not knowing what would happen next, yet knowing exactly what would happen next. It was the feeling of final drinks and saying goodbye on street corners. When would the shift arrive? In these moments I was used to feeling rigid. It was my job to be still and let them act. There were so many times I sat like this and felt my options leak away. So many times I felt I wasn't in control. I didn't want this to be one of them.

"I think," I ventured, my voice cracking the delicate silence, "it's time for bed."

"You didn't have a nice time?" His words came out icily. I could never tell when he was joking, or when he had his knife out. "What, no good-night kiss?"

"I did have a nice time," I said carefully. Seconds passed.

"Willa, *relax*. Like I'm gonna force you to kiss me or something. Jesus. Is that what you think of me?"

Yes, I thought. "No," I said, laughing a little and shaking my head. "Sorry, I'm just tired. Fun night, though. I'll see you tomorrow?" I watched the air in the room desperately, waiting for it to stop shimmering with threat.

"Fun night," he repeated, each word emphatic and mocking. "Hey, you know, I'm going out of town tomorrow. Spending the week at my friend's beach house in Jersey."

"Oh, yeah? That sounds nice." I stood up with some relief, escape in my sight.

"You wanna come?" he asked.

He must have known I couldn't. "I have to work, you know."

"You can't take a week off? I'll be back next Monday. Oh, look—the picture." He held out his phone. The photos from the night had already been uploaded, and he showed me the one of the two of us. I looked just as I hoped I had—effortless, dark-haired, and less affectionate than Ethan, with his hand making a vise around my upper arm. But we looked happy, somehow, smiling in a way that reached our eyes. I hoped he would send it to me later, though I didn't want to ask. The photographer had handed the business card only to Ethan. I looked like someone I might have wanted to be when I was younger, was what I thought—someone dressed up, in a nice outfit, with a handsome blond man on my arm, at a party where no one could tell from this frame that I didn't know a soul.

29

Durland, New Jersey, 1998

The time ticked on the bottom of the screen as we watched the crowd in Times Square. Jackets with hoods pulled up to hang over foreheads, multicolored scarves tucked under chins, everyone waving streamers and banners that sparkled, holding hand-painted signs that said things like *Hi Detroit* and *Happy 1999*. I was nine, and it was the first year I'd stayed up until midnight. "Next year you'll be double digits, so I guess you're ready," my mom said, and I glowed with the permission, of not leaving her room for my own. At that time, her bedroom felt like an extension of the living room, another place with a TV, another place where I'd lie down and put my head on her stomach, where she'd let me sprawl all day if I was home sick from school.

"Can I get dressed up?" I said. She nodded, but stayed seated on her bed. I got up and turned into her closet. She had the biggest closet I'd seen—you could take just one step into it and spin, a little square box of hanging rods and shoe racks, stained gray carpet underneath your feet. There were still a couple of my father's jackets pushed into the back. She didn't have to tell me I could take anything I wanted—it felt like her things were communal, like we shared them, like once her dresses didn't pool at my feet, I'd own them too. I emerged with a purple satin button-down shirt, with shoulder pads and a collar that pointed in two triangles. The buttons were little gold circles, and I buttoned the middle three, and then pulled up the hanging sides to tie them into a bow, like a belly shirt. She followed me into the closet, and our two bodies filled it exactly. She reached past me to take down a box of jewelry sitting on a shelf above my head and draped a strand of pearls over me, then a gold chain.

"And what should I wear?" she asked.

I knew that she was really asking. Already I loved to think about which clothes of mine matched others, to page through catalogs and fold down the pages of outfits I wanted, to tear them out and sometimes tape them into collages of what I wished to wear. But my mom was not someone who cared about appearances or clothes, or knew which shoes to wear with skirts, which socks to match under her shoes. I looked at the mess of her clothes seriously. Shoulders hung off hangers, blazers from decades ago languished on either end. I reached up and tugged on a blue sleeve. It was a fancy long-sleeved shirt that draped in three folds over her chest, and she pulled it on over her gray plaid pajama pants, the center hanging so low it revealed the crux of her beige lace bra. The shirt was the color of her eyes—after she put it on, they seemed bigger, rounder. *I did that*, I thought. Then she circled pink blush over my cheeks, let me stroke on some of her lipstick, rubbed her finger over my front teeth where I'd turned them red.

"You're going to be the life of the party," she said, watching me watch myself in the mirror. It was like she was watching me turn into a grown-up, and I felt like I already was, as she imagined a future unfolding for me with parties and glitter and rooms where people were happy to see me, champagne flutes stacked one on top of each other, tiny hot dogs and toothpicks passed on moving trays. Later, I would wonder what kind of world she'd imagined, one she hadn't lived. With our new outfits, we settled back onto her bed, lounging in the middle like we were on a float in the ocean.

The TV panned over an endless sea of people, bouncing up and down with pink cheeks and hyper hands waving to the camera. Shoulder to shoulder, jovial and sardined. My mom had poured us sparkling apple cider in her fanciest wineglasses, the ones she got from her wedding. The cup curved up from the stem in frosted-glass petals, like drinking from an outstretched flower. We sat on her bed, unmade as always, a tangle of sheets and a kicked-down comforter. We yelled the countdown along with the crowd. I flopped onto my stomach, and a slosh of apple cider darkened the sheets. My mom rubbed into it with the palm of her hand, then looked back at the screen. Times Square looked so cold and far away. I didn't know why you'd be there when you could be here. As "Auld Lang Syne" started to play, confetti streamed down on the crowds, spotlights illuminating faces and families. She ripped up a paper towel that had been crumpled on her bedside table and threw it in the air over my head. Everyone on TV looked so happy. But so did we.

30
New York City, 2014

The next weekend, Charlotte asked me to meet for lunch. She was coming to college here next year, had I heard? My dad had texted me about it. She was going to the School of Visual Arts to study photography, or considering it. Her friend's parents were driving her in to take a campus tour, and said they would drop her off to have lunch with me.

I want soup dumplings, she said. *Where's your favorite place for them?*

I read ten articles on soup dumplings before responding. On the day she'd be here, Bijou had a half day for another conference. I could have asked Nathalie for the afternoon off. Instead, I asked Charlotte if it was okay to bring Bijou. I guess I was just like my dad. Couldn't be alone with my family.

Sometimes being in Chinatown made me feel a melancholy indigo, skittish with a feather-brushed sadness. Once I saw a man hawking newspapers yell after everyone who passed, holding out the folded paper inches from their arms, but when I walked by, he looked at me and said nothing at all. Once I stepped toward a wooden crate full of the bumpy, burnished red skin of lychees, wanting a handful to peel open on a park bench. I loved their pale, smooth fruit, how the skin was a bright distraction, nothing like the meat underneath. But when I went to buy them, I got a hefty plastic bag, two pounds' worth in my hands, so much I didn't know what to do with them, so much that they took up half a shelf in my fridge. But it was the only place where I'd had soup dumplings. So that was where we went.

*

I forgot that Charlotte had always liked kids, even when she was younger. She would probably be a great babysitter. My insides ping-ponged back and forth as we waited for her, and I saw her get dropped off by a car. She waved at them as she walked away, and I waved too. She held up a hand to high-five Bijou and then ruffled her hair when she approached—two movements I would never think to make, that seemed more normal than anything I did. We went into the half-full restaurant and slid into a small booth. I sat next to Bijou, and Charlotte sat on the other side, so we were facing each other. I watched her slide in, and I thought, *That's my sister. And I've never been alone with her.* I didn't usually call her and Esther my half sisters until the second time I brought them up. When people asked about my siblings, I said I had three, and if the conversation continued, I would clarify their fractions.

Charlotte asked Bijou what grade she was in, how old she was. I watched them exchange information and noticed the ease with which they spoke. I didn't know why everything always felt harder for me than it did for everyone else.

"How was the campus visit?" I asked.

"The studios and classrooms were cool, but the dorms—minuscule! And some of them only have bunk beds. I don't know how I'd deal. Mom said that I can maybe get a single one if I submit some kind of letter about having sleep problems."

"Oh, you have sleep problems?"

"Not exactly, but having to share my space with someone gives me anxiety."

"Sure," I said. "It's not very fun." A woman dropped off menus and we pulled open the sticky laminated pages. I felt conflicted with love and its inverse. I felt like I didn't know how to speak to someone. Everyone else said whatever they wanted all the time. What did I really want to say? When I looked at Charlotte, I didn't feel envy. It was just that she didn't have the whole picture. What I wanted her to know was what it was like for me. I thought about my behavior from her point of view; maybe she wondered why I, her sister, never called, and didn't want to come home. *Because I don't have a home*, I thought. If I could have her understand anything, it was this: *Do you know the feeling of home that you have? I don't have that.* They must know how little I fit in at their house, but it occurred to me they probably thought that my *home* home was at my mom's, that that was the place where I was myself. But it wasn't, not since her new family took over. I guessed I wanted her to know that. What was the opposite of nuclear? I'd looked it up once. There wasn't one.

"So you're a photographer?" Bijou asked. I'd told her, but Charlotte also had a camera hanging cross-body, the strap looped over one shoulder.

Charlotte nodded, and maybe I did envy her that, that she could call herself something, that she could claim it. She took the lens cover off her camera. "Want to try?" she said, offering Bijou the camera. "So Dad told me that you live there, right? In Tribeca? Do you like it better than Brooklyn?"

"In some ways," I said. "Quieter, cleaner . . . everything around us is more expensive, though." It was strange for me to imagine my dad passing back facts about my life, talking about me to anyone else. Bijou studied the controls carefully, then aimed the lens at me. I ignored her and kept looking at Charlotte. She had grown taller, she had a dimple in her chin. "Where would your dorm be, again?"

"They're all over, so maybe Chelsea, Soho, Gramercy . . . I'd have to wait and see. It's so hard to choose. Oh. Dad told me that you were learning Mandarin. I started taking it this year too. My teacher says I have a good accent, but memorizing the characters kills me."

"Oh, um." I looked at Bijou, but she was taking a picture of the sauce containers on the table. "I actually stopped. Just for a little. Dad told you that?"

She nodded. I debated not saying anything, but then I did. "He didn't even respond to my text when I told him." I had tried to forget that I texted him the week before Nathalie had canceled the classes.

Charlotte rolled her eyes. "That's how he is. He never responds to anything. Here, look!" She reached for her phone, which had been lying facedown on the table. She pushed it in front of my face, where it was opened to a message thread with our dad. I resisted the urge to grab at it. They were all blue messages, sent by Charlotte.

"I mean, he literally never responds," she said, taking her phone back and placing it down on the table again. The screen transitioned to her background, which was a grainy photo of her parents—my dad in his thirties, Cynthia with lighter hair, both of them in sunglasses and short sleeves. "I'll send him a question and then I have to find him in our house and force him to respond to it, but it's like, he always already knows what I'm going to ask. Why can't he just text back? It's like you have to ask him everything twice."

The server came over and looked at us. "Um, we'll have tea—jasmine tea, and two orders of soup dumplings, one pork, one crab? And we still need to look at the menu." She walked away without writing anything down. "Sorry, is that okay?" I said to Charlotte. "Do you eat pork?"

"Love it," she said. She flipped the laminated pages in her menu. "What about the XO rice rolls and the oxtail soup?"

"I want fried rice," Bijou said, "and soft-shell crab."

Soup at a group meal, no concern of slurping, and the most expensive thing on the menu. I nodded.

"What do you want?" Charlotte said to me.

"Those are fine," I said, and closed my menu. "I love oxtail," I said to Charlotte. I did—our grandma made oxtail soup. Once she'd given me two quarts to take with me after visiting her. The broth was shimmery and lingered luxuriously on your lips.

"What are your summer plans?" Charlotte spoke to Bijou.

"We're going to stay with my aunt in California. My mom doesn't like to be here much in the summer. We used to go to the Hamptons, but her best friend got Lyme disease there."

"My mom's friend did too!" Charlotte said.

As we continued to talk, it was like Bijou and Charlotte knew each other better than I knew either of them. We finished the soup dumplings, and I pushed the last one toward Charlotte. She held out her chopsticks and lifted it to her mouth. I felt a rushing love for Charlotte in front of her here—none of the resentment and anger that colored my chest when I thought *about* her. But I didn't know how to communicate, how to show her that, so instead I found myself serving her—refilling her tea, pushing an appetizer toward her. She accepted things happily, naturally. The way that Bijou did. Take away their faces, and they could be the sisters.

When the check came, I put it on Nathalie's card. Was that all? I thought. It reminded me of my dad. How at the end of every meal with him, how at the end of the summer I stayed there, he drove me back to my mom's house, and the car ride passed silently. It was an hour-long drive, mostly on one highway and then another, and we passed fast-food restaurants, shopping malls, a movie theater, a strip mall. Nail salons, pet stores, car dealerships. I watched out the window, and my dad played jazz. Sometimes he'd read aloud the text from a silly billboard or a stupid store name, and I'd respond with an automatic, short laugh, and then we'd be silent again. In the end, he'd drop me off in front of my mom's house. He'd get out of the car but wouldn't go farther than the street. He'd give me a hug—a real hug, but how could I explain it? It never felt like enough. I watched him leave, and I always had the feeling of: *Wait, I want to try again. That wasn't enough time.*

I looked at Charlotte now. The meal had passed so quickly and I hadn't said anything real. I was supposed to put her in a cab to meet her friend's family. "Thanks so much for coming to have lunch with me," I said.

"I was thinking, if I end up at SVA, we'll be so close!"

"That's true," I said. I looked at the camera, sitting on its side on the table. Bijou had clicked around with it until the food came, and then put it down. Maybe I should have been a photographer. Something I hated about life was that there seemed to be no record of mine. That there was no proof for anything I had lived through or loved, if I went through it alone.

"So maybe if I'm here, we can meet up every month or something? We could have dinner. You can show me your favorite places."

"Oh, sure. Yeah, of course," I said. I watched her carefully—how simple it was for her to ask. She smiled back at me and I nodded again. We could meet up every month. Maybe it wasn't that everyone else was more loved, but that everyone else tried. Or that if you knew you were loved, it was easier to try. We walked out of the restaurant and down the street, passing storefronts with bags of peanuts and spices, stacked teacups and ceramic plates. Charlotte had to get in a cab, but she wanted to walk a bit, and she stopped every few blocks to frame a shot and take some photos. The streets transitioned from Chinatown to Soho—artful graffiti and expensive blazers, basement massage parlors and espresso bars. Up ahead was a street blocked off for a fair, stands set up selling scarves and incense, grilled meat and giant cups of lemonade.

"Dad always tells the story about how once you won a goldfish at a street fair when you were a kid," Charlotte said. I had a blushing memory of it, on a weekend when he had picked me up. It had been accidental, the game where you throw a ping-pong ball into a fishbowl of water, the kind that's rigged. My dad had put two arms around me and tugged me up until my feet were dangling off the ground. I'd thrown the five balls he'd paid for, and one of them miraculously went in. There was a bell, a flash of neon lights lighting up and down the stand, a commotion—I remember being scared, thinking I'd done something wrong, and then a tall man with gray stubble and a beef jerky scent handed me a plastic bag tied at the top, with a living, breathing goldfish inside. Back at my dad's house, we'd put the fish in water, and I'd watched him swim around. The next time I visited, he was gone, and I couldn't get the courage to ask my dad what had happened to him.

"That was an accident," I said. "How funny that he remembers." *He remembers.* We walked toward the fair and she took a photo of Bijou walking toward it, her hair trailing behind her. She showed it to me and I felt a twinge then, of envy. It was a good photo, the colors of the fair bright and garish, a contrast to Bijou's shiny blonde hair and pastel outfit. Bijou already was so recorded. Then Bijou said, "Can I take one of the two of you?" We stood at a street corner. Charlotte was a few inches taller than me, wearing low-heeled ankle boots. She tilted her head toward mine. The camera flashed.

31

New York City, 2014

The end of April had been steeped in blossoms, cloudy tufts of blush hanging from branches. I reached up and skimmed my fingers to the petals. Tulips planted in little rectangular prisons in the sidewalk bloomed magenta and orange and butter yellow. Restaurants put café tables outside and chalkboards up, advertising pink wine and fiddlehead ferns and outdoor patios. The air smelled sweet and earthy, tangy with sweat and skin. For one brief day toward the end of the month, the wind turned violent, ripping the petals from their branches and scattering them onto the gray sidewalks. I dug my boots around in the piles as I returned to the apartment, stopping to kick little pyramids up in the air and watch them tumble down. I was wearing a denim jacket with the sleeves pushed up, and I'd sat in the park, listening to couples fighting, and it had made me feel happy to be by myself. It was around eleven—I thought about changing into leggings and going to a yoga class or taking a book to the coffee shop around the corner. I was reading a new poet that I liked. I hummed to myself as I rode the elevator up.

"There you are, dear. Can you join me for a moment?" Nathalie was sitting at the dining room table, at the far end from the elevator.

"Of course," I said, and slipped off my boots—there was a blossom stuck to the sole, and I pulled it off. I'd ground the pale pink color off with my heel, and it was sticky and clear, like I'd squeezed out its organs. I held it between my fingers. The closest garbage was past Nathalie in the kitchen. I put the petal in my back pocket and walked over. "It's beautiful out," I said as I pulled the chair out, listened to the Lucite leg scrape.

She murmured her agreement, and once I was sitting, once I was still, she told me that we needed to talk. "About the future," she said.

*

They were going to be away almost the entire summer—Nathalie's sister, the one I hadn't met, had moved into a giant house in California and invited them to stay. Nathalie was hoping to spend less time at work. Bijou was a bit too old for a live-in nanny. I was quiet as she listed the reasons. I couldn't help but lean out of the moment and think about how it looked, how formal, that we were sitting in two seats at the end of the long dining room table, as if we were having a meeting, as if this were a regular job I was being fired from. I wish I could have a photo, an oil painting, of me here with Nathalie Adrien.

"You still have all of May here. That should give you plenty of time to find a new place and plan for the future. I'm sure you want to get started on your real life soon," Nathalie said. "How old are you now—twenty-five?"

"Twenty-four," I said, the first time I'd spoken. My birthday was a month and a half away; I was still the same age I'd been when they hired me. How did she know a real life was out there for me? I thought this job was going to help me get there.

"But if you want to keep nannying—I can refer you to some other families who might be looking," Nathalie said. "Summer and fall are the best times to find new jobs. I know one family off the top of my head, but they live uptown."

"Is this about Ethan?"

Nathalie tilted her chin at me. "What do you mean?"

"I mean . . . where is Ethan? Did he go back to school?"

"I believe he's at Katie's. I think they're back together, though he never tells me anything," she said.

I thought of the photo, the website, the women, the people there who knew Katie's name. How his arm had gripped mine as the flash went off. Our smiles. "Oh, that's good for him. Is she near Princeton?"

"Last I checked, she lived here. And Ethan's going to be staying in the city for a while. To finish his dissertation."

"Will he be staying in—the room?" I couldn't call it *mine* anymore.

"It's possible," she said. "I think it depends on him and Katie." She twirled her hair around her finger, such a young gesture. "I'm sorry, Willa, though I think you'll see it's all for the best, for you to move on."

I could feel the end of the conversation careening toward me, that what Nathalie wanted was for me to nod and agree with her, to accept the close of our time gracefully. She was giving me almost two months' notice. But still I felt hysterical, tricked. "Are you still going to have a babysitter next year?"

She breathed out. "Someone a few days a week, very part-time. Bee doesn't need the round-the-clock attention, like I said."

I could work a few days a week, I thought about saying, but I didn't. The past few weeks, the guilt I'd been carrying about trying on her dress had been replaced with the uneasiness of the night out with Ethan. I saw myself again in that dress, turning to look over my shoulder in the mirror, and in the dress I'd worn to the party, how willingly I'd played into his hand. I would apologize if Nathalie brought up the dress, if Ethan had told her. Should I tell her that nothing had happened with Ethan, if that was what she thought, if that was what his fiancée thought? *I only want to be with Bijou*, I wanted to say.

"Does Bee know?"

"I've mentioned the possibility." She looked at her nails, then to the kitchen. "I know Bijou will miss you very much, and we hope you'll stay in touch—maybe come for dinner once in a while?"

I imagined myself getting on the subway and coming here like I used to, walking in and asking the doorman how he had been. I thought of Bijou being three inches taller each time I saw her. I imagined myself bringing a bottle of wine or a little cake. It didn't seem real.

"This is another job in a series of jobs," she said. Her lips were the pink of a brand-new eraser, and they were turned up at the corners, and her hands were outstretched, as if she were offering me something rather than taking it away. She said it kindly. She said it like she thought it would help.

"Why did you hire me?" I was surprised at how easily the words floated from my lips; it felt like saying anything at all, and with it came a rush to my head like I was hanging upside down from a branch. Maybe this was what it was like to say what you had wanted to for so long.

"Hmm," Nathalie said. She put her foot up on the chair and circled an arm around her knee. "Why did I hire you? I liked you, was all. Bijou liked you. It's hard to remember exactly. You were more natural with Bee than some of the others in those first weeks—more like a friend, and she liked that." I sat still, listening to her speak. The words fell on me, and I thought distantly that they would make me happy if I weren't being fired. "We decided against having a live-in, and one of the other girls really was looking for that. So we thought we'd try you for afternoons, and then, look, things happen, Gabe's mom, we ended up needing a live-in." She paused and our eyes met. "It was always supposed to be temporary."

Each word rang through my head. If that was true, why hadn't she let me in on it? I hadn't known I was on a wheel, running out my time. I drummed my nails three times on the table, in a row and rapidly, so they went *tttat, tttat, tttat.* She looked surprised. It was something that she did. Early on, I had thought it sounded rude.

"You know—Ethan—it wasn't . . ." What could I say? He hadn't really done anything wrong. There was nothing that left a mark. I should have known by now that no one ever cared about small harms, even cumulatively.

"Ethan what?" Nathalie launched each syllable into the air like a taunt, arrows that left heat on the tips of my ears, as if she had missed, but on purpose. She had thought herself kind minutes earlier, and I should have accepted her words gratefully, each morsel of bland recognition as if it were filling, as if it were enough.

I felt stupid then, for going to the party, for buying the dresses, for walking around Tribeca with sunglasses on, as if I'd never leave. For thinking that if I laughed at some of Ethan's jokes, if I made Bijou her breakfast the right way, if I were quiet enough walking around, I'd earn my way into staying. Bijou was always getting older. Ethan was always moving in. I was always temporary. There was nothing more to say.

"Nothing. I hope he finishes his dissertation. I'd love to come back for dinner and see Bijou sometimes." I stood up, and for a second I thought we would shake hands. But she just sat there, her fingertips folded before her, the conversation finally bending her way. In the bathroom, I reached into my back pocket and pulled out the desecrated petal, and I rubbed it between my fingers, courting a soft, gummy disintegration, something that I could make happen with my own two hands.

*

Nathalie said I could tell Bijou myself, but when I went to talk to her that night, she already knew. Gabe had picked her up and brought her home and I was in the living room, Nathalie out for something. Gabe waved at me and went into his room. All this time and truthfully, I still didn't know what to call him by.

"Hey, come here," I said. I was sitting in the window nook. "Have your parents talked to you?"

She nodded. I had tried to pull her onto my lap, but she wasn't that much smaller than me, her legs, her arms. *She's going to be so much taller than me*, I thought, and I wouldn't be around to see it.

"So I'm going to be leaving at the end of May."

"I know," she said. She moved off of my lap to sit next to me on the cushion. "You can still come over for dinner sometimes," she said. From this angle, she leaned her head against my shoulder, which felt more natural. I coughed and shrugged my shoulder so she had to pick her head back up. It was like she was comforting me.

*

For a few months after I was born, my parents still lived in New York. Brooklyn, but a different Brooklyn from the one I knew. They lived in a house in Park Slope that was crumbling and a little desolate, so they claimed, though a crumbling block in Park Slope was hard to imagine now. They moved into the suburbs when I was a baby. My mom was so young, twenty-three, my dad twenty-six, and she didn't know yet how to be a mom, just that she wanted to be one. She hinted, later, that my dad hadn't been ready, but that she wouldn't give it, me, up. Sometimes I'd imagine wanting something that much, that I could want it for two.

She had emailed me a couple of weeks back, and included pictures. One was of Alex—he was eight now. Blond hair, my mom's blue eyes, fair skin, a spray of freckles across the bridge of his nose. The freckles were from my mom—I had them too, light brown dots under my eyes. He looked like my mom, but after months of staring at the Adriens, all I could think was that he could have been one of them too. But he wasn't. He was one of mine. And I barely knew him.

In the second photo, we were at the Brooklyn Botanic Garden, and I was about ten. It was cherry blossom season. *This was my favorite thing to do in the world*, she wrote. In the picture, I was on her lap and her arms were wrapped so tightly around me. We must have asked someone else to take it; there wasn't anyone else we would have been there with.

Was her favorite thing the blossoms or the park or being in Brooklyn or having me on her lap, where I wanted to be so badly, with my hands squeezing, one hand on each of her arms? I looked up the botanical garden online. Still cherry blossom season, for another couple of weeks. I'd never returned. The only thing I'd never let Bijou do. In the picture, my mother was blonde and blue-eyed and young, and her eyes didn't look as hollow as I imagined she felt, alone with a kid. I touched my teeth when I glanced at the picture, looking at how white and straight they were. I'd never had braces. Those were still my teeth.

I didn't need to open my laptop to see it. I'd had the picture framed for years. It was propped on my nightstand, next to the new books I'd bought and the lamp that the Adriens had left there. I'd told myself I kept it because of the blossoms, the nature, how cute my blunt-cut bangs looked. But I guessed sometimes I liked thinking of my mom, the way she was before. I hadn't responded to her email, but I wanted to. I wanted to know how to.

Lately, I kept having this memory of when I was younger, five, six, seven, some small age like that. My mom was sitting in the backyard, grazing the tops of the flowers with her hands. The peonies were thick and cream-colored, right below her fingers. I smiled wide for her and asked her how my teeth looked. She bared her teeth back at me in response.

"But how do they *look*?" I'd said again.

She moved in closer to examine. "Scary, like the big bad wolf. Just kidding." She said it in one monotone register. She was like that sometimes, the flame inside her blown out. I kept my mouth stretched wide, but she was looking at the flowers again, grazing the tips of the petals with her hands. I reached down and pulled out as many peonies as I could grab, but they were so wide I could only grasp three.

"*Willa*," she said, leaning forward, reaching for the petals as they scattered.

"You never check if I'm brushing my teeth," I said. "You can't even tell that they're rotting!"

I ran back into the house, where I peered out the window, waiting for her to follow. She stood up and collected the fallen petals, kneeled to examine the spots where soil had spilled. I felt terrible afterward; why had I done that? My mom loved the peonies, and they were in pieces. Was I the same person that I was then? Now what was I tearing up, trying to get myself loved?

32

New York City, 2014

It was not hard to find a new apartment in New York; all I needed was a little bit of money and a willingness to live with strangers. I fantasized about getting a studio, a small slice of a building that I could call my own, or even leaving altogether, but in the end, I went on Craigslist and answered ads. I had enough money saved up for a couple of months of rent while I looked for a new job. Nathalie had offered again the names of families she knew looking for a nanny, and I'd taken the info, but I didn't know if that was what I wanted.

Bijou wanted to see my new apartment. I'd visited places over the last week while she was at school and had chosen one a few days ago. I didn't think she'd like going into Brooklyn and visiting my new sublet, but she kept asking, so I arranged a time. I didn't tell Nathalie, but she never asked what we did anymore. My new roommate left the keys in a potted plant on the stoop.

After we got off the subway near the new apartment, Bijou let go of my hand and began skipping past the multicolored houses and the stoops with people hanging out on them and the cars that idled on the curb, music playing loudly. It occurred to me that she didn't know a neighborhood that wouldn't welcome her. "The houses are so pretty," she said as we passed a street of brownstones. "It looks like the West Village." I continued to shepherd her down the blocks until we reached my new street. We walked up three flights of stairs. "This is good for exercise," she said.

The bedroom had been vacant for a month, so we walked into the white-walled room. The previous tenant had left her mattress on the floor, but otherwise it was empty. It wasn't too small or too worn down or too big or too expensive; it was blank, and unremarkable, an empty room.

"I like the window," Bijou said.

"Are you trying to make me feel better or something?" I said.

She looked back at me, hurt. "What do you mean? Don't you like to sit in the window?" She climbed up on the ledge and curled her knees to her chest. "Like this."

"Sometimes I do, yeah." That shame—sometimes I forgot that I was in the habit of digging out meanings from sentences. But Bijou was still unfinished—new enough to still be kind.

She pointed. "Look—there's a restaurant." I craned my head to where she sat and saw that from here, there was a view of a little restaurant across the street. A man held the door open for a woman, and they went inside, bells jingling.

"I've heard of that one," I said. I leaned against the wall opposite her, tilting my head back onto the plaster, and we watched out the window. I looked down at the crown of her head, where her hair parted in the middle. I touched my palm to her hair, and she leaned her head into my palm, the movement so small that no one else would be able to see it.

We walked down the flights of stairs and back onto the street. She walked out ahead of me and down the sand-colored stoop, and I pulled the front door shut. It was bright out, the four o'clock sun high in the sky. "Should we walk around a bit?" I said. "We can look at the neighborhood." Bijou nodded, her hands on her backpack straps. Her last week of school was next week, so she didn't have much homework. Next month they were going on vacation. At first I'd thought, couldn't I have stayed an extra month, if they weren't even going to be there? But I guessed it was time to leave that cold, sterile box, high above everyone else. I took Bijou's hand, her warm, slightly sweaty hand, and we took a left. I didn't know where to go any better than she did. In that way, everything was still the same.

We took a left at the next bodega, and we passed another row of houses and a coffee shop. There was a yoga studio ahead, one room with a window that looked out onto the street. I saw a class beginning, the students unrolling their mats and sitting cross-legged on blocks. A woman came running, a tote bag hanging off her elbow, and as she rushed past us, her yoga mat tumbled from her bag. Bee spun and caught it with one arm before it dropped to the ground. "God, I'm sorry," she said and scooped the mat from Bijou's arms, and when she said this, she looked over Bijou's head and right to me. "I'm running so late," she said apologetically, and gave a little wave as she disappeared into the door.

As we circled back, we passed the pizzeria I could see from my window. Bijou walked over to the window and leaned in, shielding the sun from her eyes with her hands so she could get a clearer look. "It's supposed to be good," I said. I couldn't remember why, but that was how it was here, certain restaurants ordained, others in the shadows. I recognized another one down the street. "That one's been here longer, though."

"Maybe that one's better," she said.

We waited for the light to change at the corner. "When you get back after the summer . . ." I watched the outstretched red palm blink, *wait, wait, wait,* and then it switched to walk, a glowing white stick figure moving forward. "We can go together." I crossed the street and hoped she was next to me. "Maybe on a Monday."

I didn't know why those words made my heart pound. Maybe it was because I was a remnant from a family that didn't exist, but that both my parents were bound to. I hated to make myself feel any more like an obligation. Too scared to put someone in a position of not wanting to say yes, but having to. But what if that meant I never gave them the opportunity to accept? I would continue feeling like a ghost. I would continue feeling not wanted, but endured. Already I thought about amending what I'd said, but we reached the other side of the street and I stood still and looked down at her. She was distracted by her shoelace, but then she looked up. She said yes.

"Research," she said. "For my restaurant."

"Research," I said. It felt like that for me too.

33
New York City, 2014

The restaurant across from the Adriens' was setting up for service: the servers were folding forks into napkin rolls, straightening chairs, and arranging wineglasses and water cups at pleasing angles. I was a week away from moving out of Tribeca, but as I headed toward the subway, I felt cheered by one of the main reasons I loved New York: solitary people everywhere, having as much fun as the coupled. A girl lying alone on a picnic blanket, reading a paperback; a man with a sandwich on a park bench, chewing contentedly; a woman with freshly dried nails making her way carefully down the street. It had been a rainy week and now that the sun was out, everyone offered up their closed eyelids, the insides of their elbows, their winter-pale skin. There was a man playing saxophone on the street corner as I passed, the deep brass sound bouncing behind me.

I descended the subway stairs thoughtlessly, swiping my card and walking three cars down and sliding into an empty seat. The trains smelled warm, like bread rising, everyone's skin newly baked. I stood early, before my stop, hanging on to the pole as we swung to a stop.

I didn't know what being a nanny would entail, but what I had been thinking at the time, what I was thinking all the time in every second in which I walked through my solitary world, was, *I don't know what it's like to be in a family, and no one in my family knows what it's like to be me.* I guessed what I wanted more than anything was for someone to share my view of the universe, to step inside what things were like for me, and say it was real. So then why did I keep hunting out blank slates, people who knew nothing about me? It was so seductive, the idea of starting over. But then I'd never get to see how anything ended. I wanted the full loop.

I emerged at Eastern Parkway, the sun on my arms. Light glinted off car windows and sunglasses and gold watches on the wrists of those around me, so that everything seemed to sparkle. The day Nathalie had let me go, there had been cherry blossoms all over the sidewalk, but that couldn't be the last time I saw them this year. I knew the season was over, or had just ended, but when had I ever done something when I was supposed to? It couldn't be too late. I trudged forward, seeking out the spot where my mom and I had taken the picture. Maybe it would come back to me when I got there. I passed through the entrance of the botanical garden, the gift shop, white walls leading to paved pathways. There was a map in my hand, but I didn't look at it. I passed a group lying on their stomachs and propped up on elbows on a picnic blanket, tourists with clunky cameras, young couples walking hand in hand, and parents pushing strollers. I wanted to be open, not closed. That was what I had said to myself before I left, while I replied to her email. I hit send, and I couldn't sit still, and my feet brought me here.

I came upon a canopy of trees overhead, mostly green, their arms woven together. I felt rooted to this spot, my stance still. I looked closely at the branches. They were dotted with the remnants of candy-pink cherry blossoms. Many had fallen off and been swept away, already photographed and marveled at. It wasn't really the right time to look at them, but a few of them were still there—brashly blooming, hanging on and waiting to be seen—and I was there to see them.

Acknowledgments

I have so many people to thank, and that in itself is a gift.

Thank you to Monika Woods, for your early trust and faith in my voice, and your perseverance in finding it a home. A thousand mochi cakes to you and your color trends, for sticking with me through the years, and for being the quickest email answerer in all the land.

To everyone at Tin House, I can't thank you enough for your warmth, welcome, expertise, and enthusiasm: to Alyssa Ogi, Nanci McCloskey, Craig Popelars, Win McCormack, Anne Horowitz, Jakob Vala, Sangi Lama, Diane Chonette (for the cover of my dreams), Becky Kraemer (advocate and organizer extraordinaire!), and Elizabeth DeMeo (the first to Willa's side). Thank you to Masie Cochran, who knew how to point me exactly where I wanted to be; each time we spoke I told you, *I feel so much better!* And it was always true.

I began thinking of myself as a writer at The New School. To Robert Haller, Hilary Wallis, and Paul Florez-Taylor, my tireless and talented readers and favorites: this story wouldn't exist without you. Thank you for reading it a hundred times. Thank you to John Reed, Lori Lynn Turner, Laura Cronk, Darcey Steinke, Luis Jaramillo, Dale Peck, and my thesis group and cohort.

Thank you to all my students, who teach me so much about stories.

Thank you to the Byrdcliffe Colony, the Kimmel Harding Nelson Center, and the Plympton Writing Downtown Residency for rooms to write in and vital support. No October will ever compare to the one I spent at Millay Arts. Thank you to Calliope Nicholas, Carlos Sirah, Anne de Marcken, Aricka Foreman, Anja Marais, and Natalie Smith.

My life was forever changed by my fellowship at the Asian American Writers' Workshop. Endless gratitude to all of the staff and interns who made that possible, especially Jyothi Natarajan and Yasmin Adele Majeed. Thank you to my fellow cohort, for the dinners and inspiration: Mariam Bazeed, Rami Karim, and Yanyi.

The NYC literary community has sustained me in many ways. To those who read a draft of my work, provided feedback and comforting words, or otherwise made space for me: thank you. To T Kira Madden, Tanaïs, Katie Raissian, Crystal Hana Kim, David Burr Gerrard, Nick Mancusi, Alexander Chee, Ariel Lewiton, Penina Roth, Alexandra Kleeman, Mira Jacob, and so many more. To Emily Schultz and Brian Joseph Davis, who trusted me so early on, Michelle Lyn King, Laura Chow Reeve, Karina Leon, everyone at Joyland, and all the writers I have edited, who have taught me so much.

Hugs, karaoke marathons, and endless snacks for my expansive Kundiman family, who are brilliant and endlessly inspiring. To Cathy Linh Che who pushed me forward when I needed it, and read new drafts as quickly as if they were postcards. To Sarah Gambito, Joseph O. Legaspi, Dan Lau, and all of the staff, interns, and fellows—too many of you to name have given me what I never thought I'd find, which is community and care.

Pinky-Z Wu has rewired my writing brain, and I love them for it! To Amy Haejung, Annina Zheng-Hardy, K-Ming Chang (for always sending a postcard just when I needed it), and Pik-Shuen Fung (who I can't imagine going through the last year without).

The most heartfelt thank you to the friends who kept my head up throughout many years of writing and responded to my complaints with kindness and wine. To Raquel and Jonalyn Trisolini, Chrissie Guggemos, Amirah Kassem, Alexis Shanley, Courtney Cho, and Blair and Callie Beusman, who gave me more hours of advice and homemade dinners than anyone could deserve.

To Marcelle Clements, my first writing teacher.

To Ruth Wyatt.

To Sachie Makishi.

A boundless gratitude to my family. To Ruby and Chloe. To Gavin and Brogan. To Nai Nai, for your stories and strength. To Cory, who has dealt with a lifetime of me wanting to be near him with grace and patience (at least after he dislocated my shoulder that one time), and Oanh. Thank you, Dad. You always supported my dream of writing, and did all that you could to help me get there. Thank you, Mom. For all the books you read to me as a kid, for having the fiercest belief in me all this time.

Thank you to Dan, who plays the biggest part in cultivating a world where I have space to write, for a happiness so complete, I would have never known to wish for it. Somehow, I got it anyway with you.

Reader's Guide

1. *Win Me Something* is a searching book. In your opinion, what is Willa looking for?

2. Food plays an important role in terms of comfort, identity, connection, and more. Discuss how the author uses food in both communal and personal ways.

3. *Win Me Something* flashes back in time to Willa's childhood. Why do you think the author made the decision to show Willa's upbringing?

4. Flowers are a recurring image—what might be their significance?

5. Throughout the novel, racism and prejudice are pervading themes. How do they manifest overtly in scenes and also in subtext?

6. New York and New Jersey are both important settings—what parts of each do we see, and why do you think we are shown certain locations?

7. Mothers play critical roles in *Win Me Something*. How are the mothers in this novel portrayed and to what end?

8. At one point, Willa thinks, "I wanted to be chosen, or to choose—maybe I wasn't sure the difference yet. Just that I saw choices glimmering outside my reach, and I wanted to get closer." Have you ever felt the way she feels here? By the book's end, does Willa get what she wants?

9. Ethan's arrival to the Adriens' home can be seen as a turning point in the novel. Does he change the dynamic or reveal something that was already there?

10. Toward the end of the book, Willa says that she wishes someone would tell her what she's experienced was "real." What do you think she means by this?

11. What do you think the title, *Win Me Something*, means for Willa?

AUTHOR PHOTO © SYLVIE ROSOKOFF

KYLE LUCIA WU has received the Asian American Writers' Workshop Margins Fellowship and residencies from Millay Arts, The Byrdcliffe Colony, Plympton's Writing Downtown Residency, and the Kimmel Harding Nelson Center. She is the Programs & Communications Director at Kundiman and has taught creative writing at Fordham University and The New School. She lives in New York City.